The Adventures of Luzi Cane
The Soul of the White Dragon

Reviews

I loved the book about the White Dragon so much, just ordered the Crimson Dragon; such a special writing-skill being performed by the author!

- Cora Schwindt

Love this book! It opened me to exploring more than this 3D reality. I have had so many personal adventures since reading. Even met Quan Yin! Absolutely magical, enchanting and inspiring! Thank you Eriqa Queen!

- Sheri Reece

The Soul of the White Dragon is a vividly penned novel where the physical and the non-physical dimensions flow into one another as the protagonist explores new terrains in her life and also the edges of her consciousness. Through Luzi, we get to experience what everyday life in the midst of spiritual awakening looks and feels like. As Luzi becomes more familiar with her inner wisdom - often through the guidance of the white dragon and other etheric beings - her life transforms, reflecting her inner landscape. We get to see the joy that lies beyond a mentally constructed world: Another world, where imagination, magic, sensuality, and miracles are as natural as nature itself. A beautiful tale of dragons, elves and curious humans, especially recommended for anyone who's into spiritual awakening.

- Kim Seppälä, writer and consciousness explorer.

The Adventures of Luzi Cane

The Soul of the White Dragon

by Eriqa Queen

Series title: The Adventures of Luzi Cane
Title: The Soul of the White Dragon
Copyright © Eriqa Queen 2017
Copyright © Erik Istrup Publishing 2017
Cover art by Ricardo Robles Copyright © 2017
Published through Ingram Spark
Fonts: Palatino and Adobe Fangsong
ISBN: 978-87-92980-57-1

Genre: Fantasy

Other titles in the series:
Rider of the Crimson Dragon (Book 2)
Return of the Unicorn (Book 3)
The Truth of the Black Dragon (Book 4)
A total of six titles are planned

Erik Istrup Publishing
Jyllandsgade 16 stth, 9610 Nørager, Danmark
www.erikistrup.dk/publishing/

Contents

Elvendale

I must have slept. I wake up to the most beautiful music I have ever heard. I try to distinguish the different instruments until I find out that it is all voices, voices like instruments, not as a song. Lying on my back with my eyes still shut, I am simply enjoying the moment, feeling very peaceful.

A smell comes to me. It is not a common perfume, not of flowers or fruits, and not an herbal smell. It is neither female nor male in its expression. It is strange because I feel it is part of the music. Can a scent be part of music? Nevertheless, the smell kind of blends with the music as yet another instrument. It is incredible, and I feel very relaxed.

My arms are lying on each side of my body, with my palms against the sheet. I have a sense as if I feel grass has started to grow from the sheet and is now bumping against my palms, tickling me gently and in a pleasant way. I do not want to open my eyes, because I am afraid that it must be a dream and that it would end if I look around. I just slowly close my hands, and it feels like grasping on grass like I am lying on a lawn. I start to focus on smelling again. I must be able to smell the dirt and the grass, and I do! I cannot understand where I am, and do not remember whether I lay down on some lawn.

Now my thoughts are being distracted by a smell, and even a taste, of cinnamon. I have to open my eyes to make sure that it is not a dream. As I slowly open my eyes, I realise that I am looking up through leaves, seeing the blue sky above. The sun is shining through the leaves and makes them glow, sending rays of light down on me. I am lying on a small mound covered with grass. Tall trees are around me and, at some distance to my right a choir is making the music. Now I sense a presence to my left and turn my head. I see a beautiful, ageless woman standing, smiling at me. She moves close and kneels at my side. She has brought the smells; cinnamon, cedar tree, and one I cannot recognise.

"Coffee." I sense it more than I hear it. It is as if she is talking in my mind.

"It is the smell of coffee beans that have been dried, but not roasted, and then crushed."

"Oh, it is a dream," I say," But it's so real!"

"Your body is in in a sleep state on your bed in your flat, but your consciousness is quite awake, dear Luzi."

"Where am I then?"

"You're in Elvendale, my dear, and my name is Josela."

Her gentle smile has not left her face once. She has long, dark-brown hair. She wears a dress in light beige colours draped with a broad, brown band, and a reddish-brown cape with a hood hanging down her back. On her feet she has sandals with laces up to her knees. As jewellery, she wears bracelets with beads in green, red and white. Around the neck, she wears a thin, bronze-coloured chain with a stone eye in black, blue and white, in a bronze setting. The eye has an unusual depth to it.

"How did I get here?"

"This place is not part of your three-dimensional world. You cannot take your body here or, more correctly, you don't want to, but your consciousness can go anywhere in creation, meaning any universe and beyond, physical and non-physical."

"I don't understand. Why am I here?"

"You're invited here at this particular visit because we want to show you that there is a place and a life that are more real than what you are used to in your human life. At the same time, we'll introduce us, the Sidhe to you."

"The Sidhe?"

"Yes; in your world we're just a legend to most, and are usually called elves, but some of you know us under our real name."

"But why me? Why have I specifically been invited here?"

"You're here partly because your energy is right, partly because the possibilities in your future points in this direction, and partly because your soul, which is your consciousness, which is you, has agreed to be here, working with us."

"I don't understand anything of what you're saying, Josela."

"I think it is more than enough for now. It will take some time to sink in, and your mind must have some time to accept this event as being real."

At this moment, I feel that what she tells me is true, but I don't have any logical concepts from which to validate it.

"We bid you farewell for now, but we shall meet again."

I feel a wash of love and then the world and its inhabitants swirl into a vortex somewhere behind the trees, as it is a large painting. Now it's become quite dark all around me. I open my physical eyes and recognise my bedroom, where I am lying on my back on the bed, looking up at the ceiling.

It HAS been a dream... Or has it? As Josela said, it has been a journey of my consciousness, the real me, not the limited human awareness. It has been a total experience of senses and feelings. I feel her perfume at one in-breath but, when I take the next in-breath through my nose, the sense has gone. The smell of her perfume is not in this dimension.

I quickly take my notebook from the drawer beside my bed and write down the incident. Now I feel sleepy, and my eyes slowly close.

Lucia Cane

I wake up at eleven past seven in the morning and remember the dream from last night. For some strange reason, I have started to notice specific times, which I repeat in my thoughts, seven eleven. Maybe it is just the rhyme. I reach out and take the notebook and read the whole thing again. It is a very unusual dream indeed.

Now I remember that, two days earlier, I was watching the movie The Lord of the Rings, based on Tolkien's novels, together with my sweet friend, Cassandra. Elves played a vital part in the movie, so I assume this has caused the dream to be so real.

Interestingly enough, at the moment I am doing research on what are called "Little People," who are mythological creatures like fairies, elves, dwarves and gnomes.

In a few days I will be visiting my grandparents on my mother's side, in Hong Kong.

My parents met in Hong Kong. My father is English and my mother is Chinese. My dad was, and still is, a businessman, and my mum worked as a skilled correspondent and language secretary at my dad's workplace.

I was born in Hong Kong in 1989, grew up there, and went to an English school during my earlier years. For the first year of my life my mother stayed at home, but her creative spirit was longing to get back to work, so I am used to a nanny. It was not that I felt that she did not love me; she just had a job, as my father did.

I remember my childhood as a happy time. When one or both of my parents were not at work, they spent all their time with me and, later on, with my younger sister Anna too. Anna was born when I was six, and my mother chose to stay at home longer, and my dad brought her some work she could do at home. I was at school most of the day, and Anna still had a nanny. It was nice to know that she was there when I came home. Later in the afternoon my father would join us, if he was not on one of his business trips.

My parents always call me the light of their lives, which is why I was named Lucia - Luzi for short. Anna has been named after our dad's mother, Hannah. I once asked my parents why I was not named Anna, as I was the first-born. They both said, "You were not an Anna; you're the light of our life!" After that, I have always been proud of my name.

We were quite wealthy, but Anna and I were not brought up to focus on that. The nanny, Zhen, was treated as part of the family and was well-paid. At the same time, I had never felt that the nanny was trying to please any of us. Dad has always been good at judging people, so Zhen was carefully selected and never replaced. She was still with the family a couple of years after Anna had started at school. I have just looked up the name, Zhen; it means valuable, genuine and innocent, and that is exactly how I see her. She was indispensable, true to her feelings and acted without any hidden agenda.

The house we lived in was large and with a lot of room. It was an old bungalow supplied by Dad's company. We could have had a more modern house, but we all loved the old house with the large garden, and wouldn't have dreamed of getting anything else. Everything was of wood, mostly in light wood varieties. All walls, ceilings and floors were shining in gold when the sun shone into the rooms in the morning and the evening. I can still recall the smell of lacquer when the heat warmed it up. The smell has always given me a feeling of being safe.

We had five servants - two gardeners, two housekeepers, and a chauffeur & handyman. We did not see the nanny, Zhen, as a servant; she was much closer to us than the others, even though we had a relatively close relationship with them too. Once, at an early age, Dad told me about servants.

"It's not humiliating to be a servant. It's simply a job. All services are needed. Imagine if nobody cleans the house or washes the clothes, or if the garden becomes a wilderness. If Mum and I had to do all these things, we would not be able to go to work and do what we are supposed to do there. It's a division of labour. We serve, as well as being served."

Later I learned, by looking at others' lives, that breaking the circle of becoming what your parents did for work can be quite a struggle, if you even think of the possibility.

Grandma Hannah and Grandpa William had passed away before I moved to England. In my younger years they used to visit us in Hong Kong, and later, when Anna was old enough for a long trip, we would visit them in England. At that point they had become older and more fragile, and the last trip they made to China was when Anna became a teenager. I remember Hannah and William as two very gentle and warm grandparents, always kind and with all the time in the world, never rushing and stressed.

William and Hannah were in the trading business. They mostly traded with the Far East and India. Dad was part of the business as well, and that is how he came to live and work in China. Later, Dad expanded his business activities and joined with a few other companies. His parents' business is now part of the UK office.

I moved from Hong Kong to London in 2007, starting at the university in person. Earlier I had done some online courses, but wanted to extend my studies.

I am studying history and prehistory, with a particular interest in Marija Gimbudas' research of old Europe, ancient cultures in general, ethnographical studies, literature and journalism.

As a source of income, I work as a freelance writer for magazines, papers and on the Web. In addition to that, I work as a copy-writer and as editor of books for the university, collecting data for professors and colleges and helping them edit the materials. I also do some book writing, and it is more book writing than book selling, but there is nothing new in that.

As a tool in my work I use a smartphone but, while working, I turn off all private messages since they are a huge distraction and significantly reduce my productivity and efficiency. I do not want to be a slave to technology - it has to work FOR me. I do not use games or music on my phone to distract me and obscure my thoughts; to me it is pollution. I listen to music in my home for enjoyment, not as a distraction. You may shake your head when I tell you that I use a paper notebook as well. I use the camera on my phone quite often, a lot of the time to pick up text from various sources. I may use the voice-recorder on the phone as well. When I have to write large volumes of text, I need to use a real keyboard, since I use all ten fingers. Otherwise, production would be too slow.

At this moment, I have returned from work and am lying on my sofa, sorting things in my mind to clear it and calm it, so that I can forget work for a time.

Influencing Consciousness

I wake up in Elvendale, on the mount, but there is no music this time. Again, my senses are expanded, and not only the physical; it is as if a higher know-ingness, a wisdom without a doubt, is connecting and weaves through everything. Now I have a multi-layered perception where sounds have colours, and colours have a taste. Now I know that Elvendale is just a name Josela used to make the connection easier for me at our first meeting.

"You're right. All names here have multiple layers to them, which connect to all senses. You do not only hear the sound of the name, but you'll also smell it and taste it and, in time, you'll recognise that you have over a hundred senses."

Josela comes out of the trees. Her gentle smile and beautiful eyes amaze me once again. I feel a deep connection and warm love.

"Hello, Josela. Wonderful to meet you again. Is part of my consciousness sleeping again?"

"Let's just say that your three-dimensional human awareness is put to sleep. Right now, I would ask you to close your eyes and imagine how your body might look here in Elvendale. It can be anything!"

I imagine my human body in a long dress which is light and in various blue colours of the sky. My hair is hanging loose, and I wear a diadem with light-blue, transparent stones, some cyan and a large dia-mond in the front. I open my eyes and look down at myself and, indeed, I now wear this beautiful dress that I imagined. I reach up and surely enough, the diadem is sitting like a crown on my hair.

"I know that I don't have eyes to close in a physical sense - it is just part of my consciousness that I shut down, is that right? And how is it that it is so easy to create in Elvendale?"

"Indeed, here in Elvendale we, as the consciousness we are, create our world with imagination. This imagination triggers dormant and neutral energy, which then shapes around the blueprint that our imagination has created. There is no magic to the process, or should I say that this IS the real magic. Magic usually doesn't work on Earth, because people try to do magic from the brain. The brain does not have that ability. The steps of true, conscious creation are like this: The thoughts of consciousness are true imagination so, through imagination, a blueprint is manifested. The blueprint does not have to show a thing, but can be any concept, like events or intimate experiences. The blueprint attracts dormant, or pre-energy, and this attraction revives or activates the energies. The energy with the right attributes starts to swirl in and places itself into the blueprint, and the imagined takes form. In your three-dimensional world, you do the same thing, but most of the process is happening in the non-material realms, even the shaping. If the imagination or, as you would say, the energy, is still on the subject, the shape will be lowered into your reality with synchronicity by lowering the resonance to fit your human reality. As I said, shapes don't need to be an object, but can be of any concept, feelings, or events of any kind. Your impatience or doubt usually sabotages the creation, because you discard it as impossible and, in reality, do not KNOW that you can create. This knowingness is natural to the consciousness, while the brain or mind always questions everything. If your creation does not show up at the time or place you expected, you discard the creative process."

"I thought we manufacture things."

"In a physical sense, you do, but it starts with consciousness one way or the other. Your physical raw materials were, at some point, manifested by consciousness. Our world is not as dense as yours. Humans are taking the creation one step further and making their world solid."

In this environment, or should I say expanded consciousness, all that Josela tells me makes perfect sense. I wonder how my human part will deal with it. And speaking about the human part, I would like to know more about sensing and pose this question to Josela. "I would like to know more about sensing. How can consciousness sense things without a body?"

"You, as consciousness, have the full spectrum, or range of awareness and, when you connect to the body you connect to its limited senses. When your mind, which isn't you, is disconnected from the body's senses, you say that you're unconscious, but it's just that the mind is unaware of the signals sent from the senses in the body. When you visited us last time, you thought that you had a body because you're so used to one. You thought you smelled, heard and sensed our world with your body, but it was your consciousness that connected to ours in the world that we had created."

"Why have I, as consciousness, chosen to incarnate on the physical Earth? It's easier and much more fun to live here."

"First, I must tell you that you don't connect to your full consciousness at the moment - that's why you ask this question. Otherwise, you would know. You're on Earth to experience life in a slowed-down way to get all details out of the experience from a limited perspective and comprehend cause and effect. It is a unique way of experiencing, and this cannot be done fully in a fully-conscious environment, so to speak. At some point, we must all go through this experience. It is why we increase our contact with humanity. We want to smooth the physical environment and improve our skills before larger groups start to incarnate on the physical Earth. There are forerunners from our side, but it's tough for most of them handling the human consciousness, the physical creating procedures, since the full awareness usually fades out in the early years like it does for most humans. Sidhe, who incarnate in physical form, have a deep know-ingness that anything can manifest in an instant. They get frustrated, when it doesn't work, because they buy into the human consciousness that says, or believes, that it can't. I can tell you that there are a lot of non-physical planets like Earth, created as training grounds. A lot of humans are teaching at these places, even though they don't know it with their human awareness. They work double shifts, or even more, often at the same time, since there is no focus on your daily awareness from a large part of your consciousness."

It is fascinating, and I want to know all there is to know, but I cannot use this information in my book, so I need something else.

"I need some facts about Sidhe for my book. Could you please help me with that?"

"We're not elves and faeries like in your mythology, but the Sidhe is the basis for the stories of elves. Sidhe and most humans have a common ancestor. Faeries are derived from Gaia, the Earth, as are some of you humans. Sidhe and most people are star seeds, seeded from the Pleiadeans into the DNA. Those of the star seeds who chose to stay ethereal became Sidhe, and the ones who focused on the physical experience became humans. The humans that are not star seeds derive from the planet itself, from Gaia. We do not like to play the 'us-and-them' game. You can say that most humans have more in common with Sidhe than with the humans who have their origin in Earth, simply because we have a pre-Earth history, so to speak. All this being said, we must remember that we are consciousness or awareness, not bodies, either physical or ethereal."

"Why can't we humans sense your presence, when we're so closely related?"

"Because of the increasing focus on the physical, humanity over time lost the ability to detect the nonphysical worlds easily, and technology began to take the place of inner powers that then became dormant. Humanity is not to blame for this, since the physical experience is both addictive and demands a lot of attention. Imagine flowing down a river standing on a tree trunk, trying to keep your balance; then you have not much focus on what's happening on the banks. On the other side, imagine the Sidhe on the shores of this imaginary river. They have lost interest in the humans, who were constantly fighting to stay afloat; in the end, it seems that the two parts had nothing in common. At the same time, I must tell you that some people are aware of the ethereal worlds, but they can see that people, in general, are only focused on the physical world and what is tenable, so it makes no sense to talk to them about the non-physical world."

"Aren't there any faeries? And what about the Little People and the Giants?"

"They exist, but try to see them differently from how your mythology usually presents them. Faeries are part of Gaia, as I said before. They supported the creation of the human body until it was ready to be incarnated with human souls. They have a close connection with the animal kingdom, especially mammals, including humans in earlier times. The Sidhe have influenced some of the faeries. The Little People and the Giants are early test-models for the human body. Some of the faeries have chosen to continue taking these forms; that's why these creatures exist. The Lesser Faeries are pure nature spirits, working with nature, and then there are the Elementals, that are nature spirits as well but without self-awareness. It's not so easy to compartmentalise, since the forms are more a question of choice of shape by consciousness."

"You say that some souls come from Gaia, but from where are the rest coming? And am I, my consciousness, coming from Gaia?"

"You don't derive from the Gaia consciousness. Gaia is a collective consciousness that, for now, is working as the consciousness of planet Earth. You're a soul; YOU are from one of 144,000 angelic families existing before the creation of this universe. It is a story that has to wait until another meeting but, for now, it's important that you accept that you, the consciousness or soul, reincarnate in physical form."

"Then you have to convince me about this reincarnation thing!"

"Well, I can see that we must deal with this logically, or like a mind game. You must agree that, now and then, you meet people whom you feel you know, like or dislike, even if it's the first time you have seen them."

"Well, yes; but how will that prove reincarnation?"

"Your feelings and judgements must come from SOMEWHERE. They are experiences from other lives. You may have encountered a person who looks like this one, and you recall the pleasant or unpleasant memories, or they are someone who has the same 'energies', which means the same soul characteristics; you know the soul behind the human. The latter is usually the case if you feel you can trust this person and, in a deep way feel drawn to it."

"That makes sense, I guess. Can I call it intuition?"

"Yes, you are feeling into your soul memory, or the memory of the planet. I'll just point out that there is nothing like a so-called soul mate with whom you have to join to be whole; you're whole and sovereign on your own."

"So all humans, even those who are Earth seeds, have souls?"

"Yes; their souls derive from the Gaia consciousness, just like the rest of the Gaia entourage."

"What is my purpose in all this?"

"To put it simply, you must interject new concepts in thought patterns into the human consciousness. You're a human, already connected to the human consciousness, so your thought patterns can influence all humanity. Some individuals, who are receptive to the patterns, will take them as their own and bring the ideas into the human world."

"Is it a sort of hypnosis or brainwash?"

"No; you're just placing new ideas into human consciousness, so the ideas become opportunities for the right-minded to pick up. Only a person who is ready for the new ideas can work with them. Otherwise, they will not resonate with them."

I hear the plane's intercom, telling the passengers

to prepare for landing, and I feel a gentle hug from
Josela before my awareness is back on the plane. I
raise my seat and take a short peek out of the window. I see the sea with its islands to the south and
the sun reflecting on the water.

Hong Kong

The first thing I do after arriving in Hong Kong is to visit my grandparents on my mother's side. It is my grandma, Jiang, which means river, age 71, and my grandpa, Cheng, which means a journey, age 78. Their surname is Guan, which means mountain pass. They live in the Waterfall Bay area on Hong Kong Island, in a tiny flat.

I do not need a car here in Hong Kong, so I take the train from the airport to the East Tsim Sha Tsui Station and from here a taxi to Hong Kong Island and my grandparents' place. After the visit I will check in at Hua Qing Lou on Wah Fu Road, close to my grandparents' home.

Each time I visit my grandparents, they look much older than the last time, and every time I think that it is the last time I shall see them. Grandpa is almost 80, and a long life of work in the clothing industry has taken its toll. He could not do without Grandma, but she has become old and weak as well. They can still walk to the beach in the evening, but that is as far as Grandpa can walk.

I arrive at Waterfall Bay Road at four p.m. Grandma is sitting outside in the shade on one of the light, metal chairs at a small, square table provided by the owner of the building complex. She lights up with a big smile, which gives her face even more wrinkles. It takes some time for her to get up from the chair, so I have paid the taxi driver, got the suitcase and got to her before she gets outside the enclosure. We hug for a while, and we both have tears in our eyes.

"Welcome, welcome, dear Lucia. Grandpa is in the flat. He is not so well these days."

"Hello, Grandma, wonderful to see you."

Grandma is wearing a pale-yellow dress with flowers in orange and blue, and ordinary Chinese cotton Kung Fu Tai Chi shoes.

"I will ask the caretaker if he can look after your suitcase until you're going to the hotel. He's a nice man, Mr Wu."

Mr Wu comes out when he sees me arrive. He has a big smile on his face. "Dear Luzi, how tall and beautiful you've grown; a real lady, I should say." He wears his light-brown uniform and cap, and dark-brown shoes.

He still remembers me as a schoolgirl, even though he has seen me as an adult several times.

"Thank you, Mr Wu; I hope you and your family are all well and prosperous."

"Thank you, Luzi, indeed."

"Can you take care of Lucia's suitcase until she goes to the hotel this evening, Mr Wu?"

"Well, yes, of course; anything for Luzi. Do you need anything from the suitcase before I take it inside?"

"No thank you, I have all I need for now in my handbag, Mr Wu; and thank you for helping me out."

"Let's go upstairs. Grandpa is no doubt anxious to meet you, dear." Grandma is heading for the entrance.

Slowly we walk into the building. Luckily the flat is only on the second floor. I support Grandma under the arm. She is getting quite old. She has had a long life with many experiences, happy and sad, light and heavy. I come to think of myself when I am her age; how will my life have unfolded when I look back?

Grandpa must have heard us on the stairs, because he stands in the open doorway when we come up.

"Dear Lucia; welcome to our humble home." He spreads his arms, and we hug.

Now he takes a step back and looks at me. "You look like your mother did when she gave birth to you. Well, except for the tummy, of course!"

"Well, she IS taller!" Grandma says.

"Yes, yes, but her face. The face is as seeing Ya at that time. Am I not right? Of course, I'm right!"

"Now, go inside, Lucia needs to relax after the long flight. I'll make some tea. What would you like to eat, my dear?"

"Grandma, I'm not that hungry, but tea would be

nice, and maybe a biscuit or two."

I walk into the small living-room, where the sunshine comes through the windows, making everything appear with a golden glow. Now I have the chance to take a good look at Grandpa. He is wearing a dark-blue, loose jacket with some light patterns on the chest, over a dark-blue shirt. He wears black trousers and black Kung Fu Tai Chi shoes, like Grandma. His face looks tired, and the hair is short and grey. He places himself at the small, round dining-table, which is already set for three. It is the same china as they have always used, and all looks so familiar. The old counter, the bookshelves, Grandpa's armchair, the sofa, the knick-knacks, the paintings; I've seen it all before. Well, except for the photograph of my younger sister, from her graduation. I have seen the photograph before, but not here; I have one myself. I sit down at my usual place at the table.

Grandma comes and pours out the tea, and we talk about what has happened since we last met. Grandpa enjoys the warmth of the sun, and slowly dozes off. He is enjoying my visit in his way, listening to the two women talking, creating a cosy atmosphere.

"You should go see Ju-long. He lives not far from here. I don't have his number, but he's working at the library."

We have a local library, Pok Fu Lam Public Library, on Waterfall Bay Road just opposite a café and a mall. It is not far from my old school, Precious

Blood Primary School. I have not had any contact with Ju-long which, by the way, means 'as powerful as a dragon'. Besides, by my seeing him again, he might be able to provide me with some information now that he works at the library.

"I'll visit the library tomorrow and talk with Ju-long. It would be nice to see both him and the library again."

I stay for dinner, and it is mostly Grandma and me who do the talking. Afterwards, all three of us walk the short way to the waterfall, but not down to the beach below. Grandpa becomes more like his old self and is talking about the old days and how different things were then, like no container ships and plastic everywhere. After a short look over the bay, we start the short walk back the same way we came. I have my handbag with me so, as we return to the building complex, I get my suitcase from Mr Wu and say goodnight.

Back at the hotel, I make my arrangements for the night. I text my parents and Anna to send them greetings from Grandma and Grandpa. It will soon be morning back home. Now I am lying on the bed, sending my thoughts out, both to the past and the future.

I had a crush on Ju-long in my earlier days. I found he had more depth than most, even many of the girls. Yes, he was attractive, but he also had a subtle wisdom when looking him in the eyes, something I only allowed myself to do for a few seconds at a time.

The jet-lag has caused me to sleep longer than usual so, after a late breakfast, I am now on my way to the Pok Fu Lam Public Library. I walk very slowly and take in all the impressions, new and old. Not much has changed; mostly it is just the name and type of some of the shops, situated in the same buildings.

I arrive at the library at ten past ten. The steel shutters are retracted, and the door is held open by a wedge to get some fresh air into the room. Luckily it is not Thursday, which is the only day the library is closed. It opens all other days at 10 a.m. I walk inside and remember the smell from years back. It gives me a feeling of remembrance and safety. I walk to the counter and ask for Ju-long, as I can't see him. The girl at the counter suggests that I look into the Students' Study Room, and points in the supposed direction.

The study is easy to find, and I enter and gaze around. The only people in here are a young man, explaining something in front of a computer screen, and five young, female students, who are all focused on the young man. They all have their backs to me. I don't want to disturb them, but move closer, making my presence known to the group.

After a few seconds, the young man turns his head towards me. Can this be Ju-long? Now I recognise the eyes, and it takes my breath away. I remember him being handsome, but now he is... gorgeous.

"Luzi?"

"Eh, Ju-long?"

"Dear, dear Luzi, I didn't know you were in Hong Kong!"

"I came yesterday. I'm staying at Hua Qing Lou and visited my grandparents yesterday. Grandma suggested that I visited you, and told me that you work here at the library."

"It's wonderful to see you, and you've surely... changed. I'm kind of busy right now and will not have much time during the working day. How about we meet at the waterfall at eight o'clock this evening? It is close to both your grandparents and your hotel."

I feel a little disappointed but, at the same time, I need to have some time to get myself together.

"Well, yes, I can see that. Then eight o'clock at the waterfall. I look forward to it."

I leave the library, and I am not sure about my feelings. My stomach is full of butterflies, and it is a long time to eight p.m.

As Waterfall Road circles back to my grandparents' place, I continue following the road, but my focus is not so much what to see, it becomes more a sensing in the background. Why am I so moved by meeting Ju-long? It is as if there is some deeper connection between us. I need to find out if Ju-long feels the same way. Anyway, I am sure he was happy to see me.

I have lunch with my grandparents, and I tell them that I have met Ju-long at the library, and I shall see him in the evening at the waterfall.

Grandma lights up with a big smile. "That's wonderful, Lucia. Many couples walks to the beach in the evening. The wind is usually calm at that time, and then there is the sunset. It'll be beautiful tonight because the humidity of the air is high, and we might get some rain tomorrow."

Grandma and I are doing some shopping in the afternoon before teatime, and I have to concentrate to keep a focus on the shopping and the conversation.

"What would be the absolute best dinner we can serve for Grandpa? He is not so much in our conversation, so I want to do something special for him."

"Well I think it should be fish, then. Let's see what we can get, and then decide what to add to the menu."

Re-connection

It feels like a very long day, but finally, it is time for me to go to the waterfall and meet Ju-long. I have spent some time on selecting what to wear, and I end up with a simple, sleeveless, white dress reaching above the knees, with some blue flowers at the bottom, blue denim sneakers and no stockings. I wear my hair loose.

Ju-long is already there when I come to the end of the path close to the waterfall before the descent to the beach. He wears sneakers, blue jeans, a white T-shirt and a loose, blue jacket. His short, black hair is in a messy style. He looks very handsome or, do I dare say, hot.

He smiles. "You look breathtaking, Luzi, as always."

"Thank you, Ju-long. You look pretty handsome yourself. No wonder that the girls gather around you like flies."

"They're just some silly young schoolgirls," he says, a little uneasily. "Let's go down to the beach."

He leads the way and as I am walking behind him, I can't help looking at his nice ass. "Luzi, you are completely out of control," I say to myself.

"I haven't been here for some time. I use much of my spare time studying database programming, as well as web design."

"So, you grow up to be a computer nerd!"

He smiles, and what a smile! "It's quite interesting; they can be combined, and I can use both in my work at the library. I'm doing some freelance work in that area as well."

"Getting a little extra on the side, I see."

We reach the beach, still filled with round boulders to the sea-shore and a narrow strip of sand further up, close to the slope. Ju-long turns around and faces me.

"It's pretty stony, but let us walk, and you can tell me what you're doing for a living, Luzi."

I use the rocky beach as an excuse to grab his right arm, while we walk to the south with the water to the right and the Waterfall Bay Park to the left. The smell of rotting seaweed and algae is as I remember it from last time I was here.

"I both study and work at the university. I study pre-history, ancient cultures and social & cultural anthropology, as well as communication and journalism. The work part, where I usually gain knowledge as well, is editing books for the university, collecting data for professors and colleagues, and helping them with editing the material. I also work as a freelance writer for magazines, papers and Internet sites. I work as an editor and copywriter, and I write books."

"You have a lot of activities going on. Are you writing any books at the moment?"

"Yes, a couple actually, but the one that has my focus right now is about elves, fairies, and gnomes, in a historical and cultural perspective -why and how these stories come into existence, and whether there are common elements in stories from places far apart."

"It sounds fascinating. Now you're here, you should make some inquiries about these subjects. I would be happy to assist you, in my humble way."

"Well, I could make some inquiries at the library, but it's a vast subject if I should cover all of China. On the other hand, there must be material that has not reached the Internet, so I may find some real treats."

I feel I must know a little more about Ju-long and his life.

"How are your mother and your grandparents, Ju-long?"

"My mother is not very well. It's mainly her lungs, but she's generally weak. I live with her and her parents in a small flat on Wa Fu Road. I don't have contact with my grandparents on my father's side. My grandparents are old and not well at all. Mum's working at the mall, but it's wearing her out to take care of Grandma and Grandpa as well. It's hard for me to watch this, and I do what I can to help."

"I'm very sad to hear that. So, you're not married or have a girlfriend?"

"Oh no; I really can't afford a marriage and a wife,

and I don't feel I have the time for a girlfriend, with all my work, studies and my family. How are you doing in London?"

"I have a lovely flat and am doing all right. I have some funding through my father, and am enjoying my work and studies at the university."

"Any boyfriend?"

"No. There has been one, but we had different interests and were both very engaged in work and studies. It kind of faded away."

We talk but, after a while it was enough just to be together in silence.

We watch the sun set over Lamma Island. After that, it becomes a little chilly, and Ju-long lends me his jacket. It has a lovely smell.

We are on our way back to the waterfall, now walking through the park. Ju-long has his arm around my neck. He breaks the silence.

"I've been thinking how I can help you with your book. You should contact Ling; she is teaching at Peking University. I believe it is history and folklore, among other things."

"Ling? Really! I haven't thought of her in years, and she's teaching at the university; interesting."

"I'll find her information tomorrow so that you can contact her. I hope I see you tomorrow."

"Yes of course. Should I come to the library, or should I wait until you're off?"

"Come to the library. You can contact Ling from there. We can also talk about how we should spend tomorrow evening, right?"

"Maybe you could show me a new, nice place to eat, and then a place where we can talk, but not a cinema or such like."

He no longer has his arm around my shoulders, and I find the courage to take his hand. He grabs mine, and suddenly I feel warm all over. I can feel the connection between us. Suddenly we are standing in front of the hotel, and Ju-long takes my hands. He looks me in the eyes for an eternity.

"This is a very special moment, Luzi. It's as if we have reinforced a connection that has always been there; as if we are beginning to remember the feelings we had long ago."

"Indeed, it's almost a magical moment; yes, just as if it was a remembrance, a reconnection."

We are standing like this for a long moment, until Ju-long gives me a hug. "We'll meet tomorrow. Goodnight my sweet Luzi, the light of my life."

I am so moved, and have tears in my eyes. I am handing Ju-long his jacket. "Yes, we'll meet tomorrow. Goodnight!"

Now I'm in my hotel room, not remembering how I got here. What a special day it has been, and I'm already longing for tomorrow. I take a quick shower. The water is somehow irritating me; it is too cold and too warm at the same time. It is as if the nerves in my skin were out of order. After the shower I put on some lotion and then a loose nightgown, but then I end up naked on the bed anyway. It is a long night, but of course I doze off from time to time.

In the morning I have found my calm, although I do not feel quite rested. I take a shower and prepare myself before I go to the dining room for breakfast. I choose a more casual dress this time; still a white one with decorations, but with short sleeves. I use the denim sneakers and wear my hair in a pony-tail. There is time to visit my grandparents before I must meet Ju-long at the library.

My grandparents, Jiang and Cheng, are always up early. When I arrive, Grandpa is sitting in his arm-chair listening to the radio and Grandma is doing her stuff in their home. Grandma serves her spe-cial tea, and she and I sit down at the small, round dining-table, while Grandpa stays in his chair. I tell them in general terms about last night with Ju-long, and my plans for today - visiting him at the library, where he will help me find material for my book and connect me to Ling in Beijing.

"It's wonderful," Grandma says. "Ju-long is such a charming and handsome young man. I'm sure he can help you."

Grandpa comments from his chair, "Ling was such a lovely girl. We haven't seen her in a long time, or her parents for that matter."

I am sitting, thinking about my upcoming meeting with Ju-long, and feel like a schoolgirl in love! He has touched something in me.

"I'd better go. I don't want anyone to hijack Ju-long before I arrive."

I kiss the two old people goodbye and pick up my purse. I walk too fast, but I cannot help it; I am looking forward to being with Ju-long again; to hear his voice, enjoy his smell and just be looking at him. Just before I reach the library, I see Ju-long walking in front of me.

"Ju-long," I cry out, and start running towards him. He turns around, sees me and gives me a great smile. I reach him, and we hug.

"Hello, Luzi. You're looking fantastic."

"You too; I'm a little early, but I didn't want to risk someone hijacking you before I got here."

"I'm early, too. I wanted to get the computers up and running, so they were ready when you arrived."

Does he look a little nervous, or is he just excited to get started?

"I have the keys, so let us just get started."

Shortly after, we arrive at the library and he unlocks the security blinds, then the door, and places the book return booth at the front, now it was close to ten anyway. He is very efficient and sure of what to do.

"How long have you been working here at the library?"

"Properly, from around the time you went to England. Not full-time at first; that came later. I had to attend school before I could start as a librarian, and I've had some courses along the way, too."

We go inside, and Ju-long carries out the routines required for every time the library opens.

I follow him around, wondering why he has ended up here.

"What is it about being a librarian that you find so... can I say, inspiring?"

"Well, it's not the knowledge itself, or the stories, or whatever we provide; it's what people do with the stuff or, more precisely, what the stuff does to people. It changes them somehow, and maybe influences their dreams and choices and makes them see new possibilities in their lives."

He is deep indeed!

"That could be my answer if you ask me why I write, and in other ways provide knowledge and experiences for people. I give them opportunities that they may not otherwise have gained, or at least present a means for them to achieve those opportunities."

Ju-long has finished the usual tasks and says, "I

have some suggestions you could follow while I look up contact information on Ling. After that, I'll help you with some of the heavier Chinese literature."

"Thanks, I'll do that. It might be interesting, what I can dig up about elves and the like here in China."

Shortly after, Ju-long returns with some information on Ling, and I send her an email on her QQ-mail. Now the girl I spoke with the other day at the counter arrives. Her name is Liling. We say hello, but after that she pays us no further attention. Now visitors and other staff members come, and soon there is the sound of people being busy with their stuff. Through out this morning we are able to find some "beings" I could use parallel to the English terms through the description, but often elves and fairies are seen as one and the same creature in English, and I am not so sure myself.

It seems that elf, fairy, genie, ghost and spirit are all written as 精灵 in simplified Chinese, and pronounced "jing ling". I need to find out more about these creatures so that I can distinguish between them. It does not seem as if there were any thorough studies made of folklore creatures, except for the dragon, of course.

At Ju-long's lunch break, we go to the Howard Johnson Restaurant a little up the street and buy our lunch. It is more like a small café, but Ju-long says that the food is good. We bring the food outside and, close by we sit down on some benches.

Ju-Long finishes his first bite and says, "Well, this

morning I tried different shirts and T-shirts, including a white one with a big, red heart with a white text saying "I LOVE YOU". Then I felt it was too silly, so I ended up with this one."

It is a light-blue one, with two white swans swimming. Ju-long should know, that I do not mind what T-shirt he is wearing, if any.

"If you just knew how my night and morning have been. I WAS SILLY! Meeting you again has turned my feelings upside down, if one can say that. The T-shirt is fine; I like it. To me, it sends the same message, and I don't want to hide my feelings for you, either. On the one hand, we've just met, but on the other hand, we go way back. We're falling in love, but the actual connection has been there all these years. I love you too, Ju-long. Maybe it's not the most romantic place to say these words, but that's the truth, nevertheless."

We both stand up and hug for a very long time. Everything turns and, for a moment, the outer world is just a dull feeling somewhere far away.

We sit down and maintain eye contact most of the time while eating. It is a magical moment with much intimacy. Ju-long's phone beeps; it is time to go back to the library. We hold hands on the way back, and neither of us touches the ground.

When we are back in the library someone needs Ju-long's expertise, so I follow some of the leads gathered this morning but, honest to say, I have no focus at all. My brain is floating in a sea of hormones, completely in a limbo. I check my email to see if

Ling has answered, but there is nothing yet.

Inside, I become more and more chaotic. Thoughts and feelings are all swirling in a giant maelstrom, and I have absolutely no focus on anything.

I check my email again, and this time there is a short message from Ling. "It's lovely to hear from you, Luzi. It's funny that we should both end up working in history (and other things). I could dig up some material and send it to you by email, but we wouldn't have an actual dialogue on the subject, and there would be some waiting time between emails. I prefer you to come to Beijing and, indeed, I would like to see you again!"

I feel that I need to think this through, or rather, feel it through, because I hate to leave Ju-long just when I have found him... again. My life has completely changed, and I need to reconstruct everything, since I must stay with Ju-long. How will he fit into my job and studies in London? I write back to Ling, "Thank you for your answer. I'll find out if I can visit you in Beijing."

I must talk this through with Ju-long, and leave the study. He comes towards me. "Is there any answer from Ling?"

"Yes, and she would like me to go to Beijing. But you see, I don't know how my life is changing now that you have dropped into it, as a joker, so to speak. It has really more to do with you and me than Ling. I'm very confused; I live in London and you here in Hong Kong, and I can't think clearly."

"Let's take one thing at a time. We've found a connection, and that won't go away wherever we are, together or apart. Let us give ourselves some time to find out how we can be together. We cannot rush this. I want to be with you, don't doubt that. I think you should visit Ling at the university in Peking and see what material you two can dig up for your book. You don't leave me because you take a short trip to Beijing; it's just a trip."

"Of course; silly me."

"There is no 'silly me'. You've recognised something precious and are afraid of losing it, but you won't. Let's find some flights to Beijing and see which one suits Ling."

It makes me calm down; now I have to focus on only one goal. We sit down at one of the computers in the study. I lean towards Ju-long and feel happy and warm inside. Shortly after, I send some dates to Ling. I ask her to reply to Ju-long as well, since my grandparents do not have an Internet connection. Slowly, I can feel that everything is going to be all right and that Ju-long and I will find a solution to being together in the future. The time is now nearly seven pm, and the library is about to close. I will dine at my grandparents and Ju-long will visit us later, as is his wish. "It's a long time since I've talked to your grandparents."

We walk from the library, hand in hand and, before we part, we hug and I put my head on Ju-long's chest and feel happy. Before he leaves, he kisses me on the forehead, and I definitely want to kiss him

on the mouth, but the time for that will come. We
wave goodbye.

Ju-long

I arrive at my grandparents. The dinner is ready, and Grandpa is setting the table. "You must be hungry after such a long day."

There is a pleasant smell of Grandma's cooking, and I realise how hungry I am. "We had lunch, but now I'm ravenous."

Grandma places a big bowl on the table. "Did you have any success today at the library?"

"The actual information is a little scarce, but now I'm in contact with Ling in Beijing, at Peking University where she works. She wants me to visit her. She teaches history, among other things. Ju-long and I have emailed her some dates, and now we're waiting for her response."

"Oh yes, Ling. Funny that she is working in history, just like you."

I place a jug of water on the table, and we sit down. "Ju-long is visiting us tonight. He hasn't seen you for a long time, so he suggested coming."

"But that is wonderful, dear Luzi. We'll very much like to meet him!"

Shortly after dinner Ju-long arrives, bringing a small box of chocolates. He receives a warm welcome from all of us. Normally Ju-long would not hug me, for traditional and cultural reasons, so I give him a warm hug and hold his hand for a moment. I can feel that he is surprised but, being half English, I do not have these reservations, and I know that my grandparents will accept my behaviour. I am so happy to be near him, to feel and smell him again, even though we have only been apart for a few hours.

"We haven't seen you for a long time, Ju-long," Grandma says, and winks at me, signalling that she knows how I feel.

We gather around the small, round dining-table; I get the teacups and Grandma brings the tea. "How are your family doing, Ju-long?"

Ju-long tells us about his family. He has already told me most of it, but when he comes to talking about his parents, it is quite difficult for him to talk about his father. He has become mentally ill and has no recognition of his family. For the same reason, there is no relationship on behalf of his father's side of the family. Shortly after, he feels that he must leave.

"It's time for me to leave now. It has been a wonderful evening, and it's so good to see you again."

"I'll leave as well. You can walk me to the hotel, Ju-long; it's only a few minutes."

Even though I long to be with him, I do not want it to be a night at a hotel in secret, and we would not be able to hide it anyway, since Ju-long could not get to my room undetected. We walk hand in hand without talking, just enjoying the brief moment before we reach my hotel. Just a small sign in Chinese letters gives the name of the hotel - Hua Qing Lou. The smell of food from the kitchen ventilation is still prevalent, and the dim light shows you that you will not find a five-star hotel behind the dented door. Now we stand face to face, looking into each other's eyes. We kiss. The excitement rushes through my body, where every sensory receptor is open to taking him in. There is no time, no space, just sensory awareness. We slowly pull away from each other; we hold hands, and again our eyes meet. It is the real magic of life.

"I'll contact you tomorrow when there is an answer from Ling. Sweet dreams to you, my lovely Luzi."

"Likewise to you, dear Ju-long. I fear that the night might be sleepless, but I don't mind, since I'll be thinking of you with every heartbeat."

I can feel and see his reluctance to leave, but there will be other times, other places, and I walk through the door to find my room, just wanting to lie on the bed and float with the euphoric feelings of joy I still feel in my body.

I got a good night's sleep and now, on my way down for breakfast, I feel refreshed and joyful. The dim light in the dining room could not take away the bright sunshine in my tummy. I have decided to spend more time with my grandparents, now that I supposedly will be leaving for Beijing soon. I have no doubt that Ju-long and I will find a way to be together, so I have made the decision not to trouble my mind trying to find a solution, which will present itself anyway.

After a breakfast of mostly fruit, a little bread and tea, I leave the hotel and head to my grandparents. I know that Ling will contact me on my phone or Ju-long on his email, so there is no more for me to do in that regard.

My grandparents have, of course, been up for hours. Grandma and I agree on taking a walk and doing some shopping, while Grandpa chooses to sit in front of the building, looking at the life unfolding here, while talking to his friends.

Grandma and I have just left the mall when my phone rings. I can see it is Ju-long calling. "Hello, Ju-long; any news from Ling?"

"Wonderful to hear your voice again; yes, but I can see that you're a little pushed for time. In a few days, Ling will leave with some of her students for a two-week scientific excursion to an old archaeological dig, and is in the middle of packing. However, she would very much like to see you and, as she has studied both Seal and Oracle signs, she is most likely the best person to help you right now. You'll have to leave tomorrow, probably on business class, if you don't want to wait until she comes back. There will be a flight tomorrow, but it is not on our list since we couldn't have taken into account that she would leave shortly to the dig site. I think you should use this opportunity and get to Beijing tomorrow."

"Grandma and I are out shopping, but I'll come to the library as soon as possible and order my flight.

You and I can have lunch together afterwards."

"Sounds great; and Luzi, I love you!"

"Love you too." Warmth flushed through my body. We break the connection, and I tell Grandma the situation.

"Don't worry about me. The shopping bags are not that heavy, so I can easily take them back home. You just order the flight, before it's sold out!"

"Let me at least take one of the bags."

"Oh no; with the trolley I'll just be fine. It's better that way; and say hello to Ju-long for me, dear!"

"OK, but I don't know when I'll be back."

"We'll see you when we see you. Have a nice day, dear."

I leave Grandma, and have to stop myself from running but, shortly after, I arrive at the library. Ju-long is in the central area. "That was fast, Luzi!"

Briefly, our hands touch as we walk side by side to the computers. Shortly after, the booking information comes out of the printer, and I can relax. Now I only have to pack, which will take only a couple of minutes. I send a short email to Ling containing the time of my arrival. I will stay at Ling's place, since it will only be for a short period. She has already done most of her personal packing, and spends most of her time at the university over the last preparations. Now I need to talk to Ju-long about our future together, and we place ourselves with a book in the study area.

"Due to my dad being a businessman, travelling a lot, the whole family have been with him on some of his trips where he could combine his work with a short vacation with his family. I have papers allowing me to travel almost all over the world, so I think we could start a life together here in China."

"I've been thinking a lot about our life together too, and maybe I can get a job in England and you can continue your job and study at your university."

"It might work out, Ju-long, but you must have a job that you care for, and that might not be so easy to find."

We are both very excited about our lofty plans, and the girl at the counter has to remind Ju-long about his lunch break. We have lunch at a small café, after which I walk to stay with my grandparents.

I do not recall much of the afternoon but, after dinner, I say goodbye to my grandparents, wishing them well and then I meet Ju-long at the beach. I have very conflicting feelings, not about Ju-long, but the whole situation, and I say goodnight to him at the hotel entrance with a deep feeling of not being willing to leave him.

My flight to Beijing is very early next morning. It is an uneventful journey, done in a haze of thoughts and feelings.

Beijing

I go directly from the airport to the university where we had agreed to meet. Ling is busy instructing her students who will accompany her to the excavation site. She is firm but, at the same time, she is not speaking down to her students, and it seems that they have a genuine respect for her.

Ling is a tall, skinny woman with glasses, dressed as if her focus never was about what to wear and how to look in general. She is kind, but now and then quite distant.

We do not have much time, since Ling will leave in two days so, now that Ling has given her students a tea break in the afternoon, we are sitting in the canteen with tea and biscuits. Ling grabs a notebook and a pencil and draws two Chinese glyphs. "It's interesting that you ask ME about elves and the like. My name, Ling, means spirit or soul, or bell or chime."

灵 spirit, soul.

铃 bell, chime.

"I used to think of my name as meaning The Voice of the Soul."

In my emails to Ling, I've given a short description of what I know about Sidhe, and now I elaborate. I hope that by giving her more words, her memory will be triggered, helping her to find more clues.

Ling is sitting quietly, concentrating on the information relayed to her, searching her inner database for relevant data. When I finish, she starts using her notebook again.

"We use the glyph, Xian, for an elf and creatures like that. The ancient or traditional glyph looks like this:

"It means transcendent or immortal. If we just look at the two parts, left and right; we have a person to the left and 'soar like a bird' to the right. You may also recognise the 'spirit' part as the two top signs to the right.

亻 - Rise, a person.

䙴 - Soar like a bird.

"Other meanings can be an enlightened person, Christian and Christ. The simplified glyph looks like this:

"Again, the person is to the left, but now there are three mountain peaks to the right - the human mountain."

Is this a coincidence, or is this the proof to me that the Sidhe work and influence people all over the planet? Sidhe want to be seen as part of the Earth, and not part of the Heavens. They are not more ascended than humans, they just have a different path and a different connection.

"Interesting, since elves or, as I've learned to know them, Sidhe, are said to be living in hills, mounds or mountains; a human mountain, or a person from the mountain - a connection with Earth."

Now I see that Ling is turning to her inner database. I'm sure that she can just tell me what she knows in general, but it is as if she wants to be sure that all she relays to me is the truth, the whole truth (of her database), and nothing but the truth... so help her God. It takes only a second or two; then she's back.

"When I wrote the name of the glyph, Xian, I used

the Pinyin phonetic system; but, if I use the Wade-Giles system, it would be 'hsien', which looks a little closer to the Irish spelling, Sidhe; just a thought."

"I haven't thought of the similar pronunciation because the two words come from worlds apart, so to speak, but you're completely right!"

Ling helps me fill out a comparison list, which I have made earlier.

English terminology		Chinese terminology	
Common ancestor (star seed)	Human	共同的祖先 (星种子)	人类
	Sidhe		仙 (Xian)
Gaia (Earth seed)	Sidhe influenced Faerie	盖亚 (地球种子)	影响的仙精灵
	Faerie (the Giants + the Little People)		精灵 (巨人 + 小矮人)
	Lesser faerie (pure nature spirit)		小精灵 (纯自然精神)
	Elemental (nature spirit without self-awareness)		元素 (无自我意识的自然精神)

As I have already found out, it's hard to match them. In the evening, at Ling's place, she comes up with a suggestion.

"You are visiting old school friends. I have some

connection with Josephine Wen; she lives in Shanghai. She's working in a publishing house, and does some intensive work on old texts as well. It may be a good idea to pay her a visit, or at least make a request via email."

"If you have her phone number, I'll text her to find out when she has time to talk."

I add yet another name to my address list and start to type a short, but hopefully understandable message to Josephine.

In the evening Josephine calls me. "You really must visit me, now that you're in China. You remember Grandma? She's here too, and she'll be very pleased to see you again."

After some additional communication with Josephine, I prepare for yet another flight, this time to Shanghai.

Two days later I am leaving Beijing, and so are Ling and her students. We are not on the same plane, since they are heading west to the Xinjiang province, but I get a lift to the airport with their bus. At the airport, we say our last goodbyes and we promise to stay in touch.

Shanghai

I arrive in Shanghai at Hongqiao Airport and take a taxi to my hotel. In the evening I will meet Josephine and her husband, Ping, outside the zoo, where he is working part-time as part of his MSc in Veterinary Science.

Josephine has wealthy Chinese parents, but she went to the same English basic school as I did. It was necessary from her parents' view that she had social relationships with other children, even though they could easily afford a private teacher.

At 6 pm. I arrive at the Shanghai Zoo and find a nice place near the Elephant Gate, which leads into the zoo itself. It consists of two concrete elephants making an arc with their trunks.

Shortly afterwards, Josephine steps off her bicycle and slowly approaches me. She is obviously not sure if it is me, but I clearly recognise her, since she has not changed much from when I knew her in school. It is mainly due to her face, which is still round like a child's. The face is pretty; she is not tall and she is a little chubby. Her black hair is short, and she wears a hair slide with flowers. She dresses in a red sweater, tight blue jeans and red sneakers.

"Hello, Josephine."

"Hey, Luzi. I wasn't sure it was you."

"It's me all right."

"Welcome to Shanghai, the Crown Jewel of China."

"Sorry to say, but I feel more at home in Hong Kong, in particular on the island. The contrasts here are scaring me."

"I've got used to it, or maybe I just have learned to shut some feelings out. I hope Ping will soon come out; I'm starving!"

"I had something to eat on the plane, but it was hours ago, and I could use a bite or two myself."

"Oh, here he comes!"

She waves to a young man who is coming out from behind some trees. He is waving back, smiling. I may have had the preconception of a young, good-looking guy with a slender body, but that would not describe Ping. He appears chunky, with black hair that is little too long which cannot hide his stout face. He looks friendly, even jolly, and not capable of killing a fly. Josephine would not fear anything from him, and that may be part of why she has chosen him as her husband. I will not judge her on her choice; our past gives us all different reasons for our choices later in life. Ping wears a short, fawn jacket over a black T-shirt, and wears black trousers and sneakers. When he reaches Josephine, he gives her a quick kiss and turns to me.

"You must be Luzi; welcome."

"Hello Ping; how is work?"

"Well, dirty and smelly most of the time, but to be

with the animals makes it all worth it. Let's go for some dinner - I could eat a horse!"

Josephine turns her eyes to the sky. "You can always eat a horse. Let's just go to Delicious; it's close by, and the food IS quite good. We have to cross the road further to the right."

While we walk to the restaurant it is too noisy to talk about my real errand in Shanghai, so we just make some small talk. The noise reduces a bit when we get inside and, after ordering the food and drink, I can explain my story in greater detail. Ping does not show much interest in the subject, and his thoughts kind of drift off while he concentrates on the food. I show Josephine the glyphs I have discovered with Ling, and we have a discussion about ancient beliefs and understanding of the world.

After finishing dinner, we go outside. On our way to the sub-station close by, we plan that I will meet Josephine during her lunch break the next day. Meanwhile, she will investigate the 'holy person' for a possible connection to Sidhe.

Now I am back in my hotel room, and call Ju-long just to hear his voice. I miss him terribly.

"Hi, dear, I'm in my hotel room in Shanghai, after meeting Josephine and her husband, Ping, and having dinner with them."

"It's good to hear your voice again, sweet Luzi. I miss you so much!"

"And me you."

"What did you learn today?"

"Well, not much, but I am meeting Josephine tomorrow during her lunch break. She will probably
have something for me then if she can find the time
during her work."

"I don't suppose you know when you'll be back in
Hong Kong?"

"No Ju-long, but I don't want to stay here any
longer than necessary. Shanghai is much different
from Hong Kong, and the places I've seen so far
don't encourage me to live here. There may be nice
places, but I just haven't seen them yet."

We talk a little more, but soon there are no more
words to say, just the longing, and we say goodnight.

This evening I am not in the mood for writing. In
fact, I am not in the mood for anything. I feel that
I should do SOMETHING, but I really can't focus,
so I end up staring at the ceiling without being able
to focus on the uniform, white surface. Soon after,
I fade off to sleep.

The next morning, after a shower and breakfast, I
am much more energised and able to get quite a
lot of writing done. Later, on my way to meet Josephine at the publisher, I buy some fruit for my
mid-morning snack. I arrive shortly before Josephine's lunch break, at her work. I walk to the counter and announce that I am waiting for Josephine
Ruan. While waiting in the reception area, I am
sitting looking at the life that unfolds in the street

outside. The large windows give me a good view and here, around lunchtime, there are a lot of people moving in both directions on both pavements. There are no street traders in this section, so people use the many restaurants and cafés that squeeze in between other shops, workshops and offices of all kinds. Shortly afterwards, Josephine comes out to reception, and we leave for a restaurant where she usually has lunch. At the restaurant, after we have ordered our meals and found two seats, Josephine pulls out her notebook from her bag.

"In my search for connections to Sidhe, I've found something that might interest you. The glyph for dragon is called 'Long', and the simplified form looks like this:

"If you're not using or working with the glyphs, it wouldn't tell you much. It's easier when you look at the traditional glyph, which looks like this:

"Here it's easier to see that you, to the left, have a person. The dot above shows us that it is an individual of high status; could even be divine. To the right you see the dragon, the head at the top and the tail that curves at the bottom."

Just like the symbol for the Sidhe is a double glyph having a 'holy person', the same is the case for the dragon.

"It's interesting to see that the dragon does not have a symbol of its own, so to speak, but is flanked by a higher being."

Josephine, who feels attracted to dragons, has become excited about this thought.

"Yes, the double glyph might show that the dragon is not important by itself, or that there is more to the dragon that just the beast."

For my part, I am a little confused that this creature appears in the scene.

"It doesn't seem important to bring dragons into this investigation. The dragon is a mythological creature, which does not appear with elves and the like in Irish folklore."

"Dragons may not be a tradition in Ireland particularly, but that doesn't mean that dragons and elves do not appear side by side in China due to the long history of dragon worship."

"You're right, Josephine. Maybe I'll be able to find a relationship between the Sidhe and snakes instead. I'll try this lead with my English stuff."

"And I'll try to dig more into the Sidhe/elves direction and contact you later."

We talk a little more before Josephine has to return to her work. I use the rest of the day sightseeing in Shanghai, and find many beautiful places in this enormous city. When I am back in the hotel, preparing for returning to Hong Kong, Josephine sends a text message that she has found something of great interest, and asks me to visit her at her grandmother's place tomorrow. We arrange to meet after work at the publisher, and we take the subway to her grandmother's.

As I am heading for the publisher, I am not that expectant. In the reception area at the publisher, Josephine shows me her latest discovery.

"I found this glyph in the ancient Seal script. The dragon looks very much like the one in the traditional glyph, but look at the person!"

"To the left, I clearly see a person with a halo above the head and, to the right, we have the dragon. Is this parallel to St George and the Dragon? If so, then that story has a whole different meaning. The person even has arms, and it looks like it's a woman in a long dress! Could this prove the connection between the Sidhe and the dragons? Or is the divine person there to tell us that dragons are beings with souls and consciousness, and are not beasts?"

"Usually it's seen that the dragon gives its strength to the human, but it could as well be the other way around; namely, that it is the consciousness that is embodied in the dragon."

Here you can see the comparison list with the dragon added:

English terminology		Chinese terminology	
Common ancestor (star seed)	Human	共同的祖先 (星种子)	人类
	Sidhe		仙 (Xian)
Gaia (Earth seed)	Sidhe in-fluenced Faerie	盖亚 (地球种子)	影响的仙精灵
	Dragon, Gaia + Sidhe		龙，盖亚 + 仙
	Faerie (the Giants + the Little People)		精灵 (巨人 + 小矮人)
	Lesser fa-erie (pure nature spirit)		小精灵 (纯自然精神)
	Elemental (nature spirit without self-aware-ness)		元素 (无自我意识的自然精神)

We arrive at the building where Josephine's grandmother lives. On the way, she has told me that her grandfather died some years ago.

A Cat Called Dragon

"What is your grandma's name?"

"It's Ling, like Ling in Beijing, which means 'spiritual being'. Her surname is Bai, which means 'white'."

"Hmm, then I'm going to visit a white, spiritual being."

Josephine presses the doorbell, and we hear faint footsteps in the flat. The door-handle moves and the door opens. A small, old lady is standing in the soft light from a rice-paper lamp above her head. A smell of cooking catches my nose - curry, cooking oil and…cake.

"Hello Grandma;" Josephine gives the little woman a warm hug.

"Hello dear; and you must be Luzi; welcome."

"Hello." I give her a gentle hug, afraid of harming the fragile body.

"Come in, come in, dear girls. I'll prepare some tea for us. Josephine dear, set the table, and there is some cake in the box."

"Show me where the dinner set is, and you can prepare the cake," I say to Josephine.

"Oh, you can see the china in the cabinet through its glass doors over there."

When I walk over to fetch the dinner set, I see a long-furred, white cat, lying on a small, old sofa, staring at me with its blue eyes. The stare is very intense, and I cannot take my eyes off these two light-blue eyes that almost drag me into the soul of this small creature.

"This is Loong; it means 'dragon'," Mrs Bai says.

"Well, he sure doesn't look like a fierce dragon to me, but he's so cute and fluffy! He has a very intense stare. It is a male, right?"

"He is a male, as you intuitively knew, right? So you think dragons are scaly, have wings, lay eggs, and spew fire! Real dragons look so much like cats that you usually can't tell the difference. They even purr like cats."

"Well, Loong sure looks like a cat to me, except maybe for the blue eyes."

"Loong can be both fierce and gentle; both masculine and feminine. Don't forget that the female energy can be incredibly powerful too!" She points at me with a thin finger then, moving the pointing finger to the drawers under the glass doors, she continues: "You'll find the spoons in there; and the palette knife as well."

I decide not to go and talk to Loong right away. I'll give him some time to get used to my presence. We sit down at a small, round table with a tablecloth with a traditional Chinese motive, a little like some of the paintings my mum is creating.

Mrs Bai pours the tea, and Josephine hands me the dish with three slices of Chinese steamed cake.

"Loong is a very remarkable cat. He is observant of what is going on around him, and I believe he understands all you say to him. He is very gentle, and he loves to play, even though he looks pretty lazy right now. I can't help loving him."

Mrs Bai takes the last piece of cake off the dish.

"Since my husband died, Loong has been my true life-companion. I have learned to know what he's saying, even if it is without spoken words. I've learned to trust that what I feel he says is truly what he says. You may think that I'm just an old woman, and you'd be right."

Now I feel a strong impulse to tell about the dreams I had concerning the Sidhe. Both Josephine and Mrs Bai listen intently, and suddenly I can feel Loong brushing against my legs. I put down my hand and he bumps his nose against it; his message is, "You're dearly loved." I feel much moved, and get tears in my eyes.

Mrs Bai looks down at Loong. "Yes, he's a real charmer, and he loves you."

Josephine looks at me, not quite sure what to say.

Mrs Bai looks me straight in the eyes. "There is certainly something going on here. I suggest you lie down on the sofa for a bit. It is not something that your mind need be involved with."

I suddenly feel exhausted, and walk over and lie down on the sofa. I close my eyes and, a few moments later, I open them again and realise that I am in Elvendale. I sit up and look at Elvendale City from across the lake on an elevated, grassy land. This time I am aware that I have a body, an elven body, and I am dressed in a beautiful, long, sky-blue dress, light as the warm wind that blows it in ever-changing shapes so that it looks almost like blue smoke or flames. I hear a subtle purr to my right and turn first my head and then the rest of my body, and find myself staring at a white dragon, sitting on the long grass next to me. Its fluffy fur moves in the warm breeze. I know for sure that it is Loong. I stand up and walk closer to him.

"Dear Loong."

"Dear Lucia."

"So you ARE a dragon!"

"Well, I'm a soul, a consciousness like you. Right now, I appear like people think dragons must look. Well, maybe except for the fur instead of scales. People cannot have dragons from their folklore be seen walking around, so we usually choose the shape of a cat. Cats are known to be individualists and, at the same time, willing to interact in an intimate way. It means that we can keep a distance when it suits us, and we can get close when it is needed. Another thing is that we can stay out all night, doing our things."

"And what are your things, then?"

"It is as difficult to explain in human terms as it is for a human to understand, but I'll try, because it'll be a part of what you'll be working with."

Just now, I realise that Loong has not been moving his mouth when speaking, and I've only been staring him in the eyes all the time. "I'll do my best to comprehend."

"As you heard earlier, Sidhe and humans are now sharing experiences, with the goal of creating a common future; a future where the physical and the non-physical are joined in one reality or, more correctly, they'll be living in more realities at the same time. Still, there are only a few connections between our people, but the more people open themselves to the possibilities of a non-physical world, and Sidhe find the courage to embrace the necessary step of gaining experience in the physical, the more energy and consciousness will flow through the two realms. This flow will then give even more momentum to the process."

"How must I work to facilitate this reunion?"

"We'll have more meetings, so you'll slowly get this knowledge; but I'll tell you, as Josela also did, that you, as a human, have easier access to human consciousness than the Sidhe do, so you'll be a bridge between the realms. For now, we'll return our focus to Mrs Bai and Josephine."

"First, I want to give you a big hug. It will be the first time I've hugged a dragon!"

I put my arms around his strong neck, put my

cheek to his, and bury my hands in his long, white, soft fur. Now his love washes over me, and I am overwhelmed with gratitude and honour for this mighty soul.

The shift is very fast and I just open my eyes, finding that I'm looking right into Loong's blue eyes, now as he appears as a cat. Mrs Bai and Josephine are sitting close by, and Mrs Bai smiles gently at me when I turn my head towards them and sit up on the sofa. Josephine fetches a glass of water, and I tell them of the incident I have had with Loong.

"So, Loong is a dragon!" Josephine said, and looked intensely at Loong.

"Of course he's a dragon, dear; hence the name Loong!"

"Well, Grandma, he wouldn't be the first cat with that name, would he? Tomorrow I'll search the different scripts to see if there is any relationship between cats and dragons."

"I'll be leaving for Hong Kong tomorrow afternoon, so I hope you might be able to find something for me. The situation has taken a new turn."

"I'll start searching tomorrow the first chance I get. There MUST be something in the old scripts you can use."

We stay a while longer, but I feel exhausted and want to go back to the hotel. Our paths separate at the subway station after a warm hug and best wishes for the night.

The next morning, I check out early from the hotel and place my suitcase in a locker at a Metro station. While I am roaming Shanghai, Josephine sends me a text message.

"I've found something you must see. I won't spoil it by telling you here."

I reply that I will be at the publisher shortly. When I arrive at the reception counter the girl calls Josephine, and she comes out with a printout which she hands me.

"Hi, Luzi. I have found this glyph in the ancient Oracle Bone Script representing the dragon. Here there is only one symbol!"

I take the printout and look, very surprised at the glyph that stares back at me.

"Does it look like a cat, or what?!"

I am staring at a sitting cat with pointed ears, its tail curved forward, looking at me with big eyes.

"Well, to me it looks nothing like a dragon at all. I wonder why that is?"

"As the same Latin letter may look very different, so do the glyphs. This one has the most resemblance to a cat."

With this last piece of the puzzle on this trip, I say goodbye to Josephine, pick up my suitcase from the locker in the Metro and take the train to the airport. At last I was going back to Hong Kong, to my grandparents and, not least, to Ju-long, my strong, private dragon.

Questions to Loong

Settled in my seat on the plane, I doze off shortly after we reach cruising altitude.

A brownish haze dissolves into a myriad of colours, and becomes Elvendale; Loong is sitting close by at the tree-line between the grasslands and the extensive forest further inland. I more glide than walk to him, and he greets me with a warm feeling of love.

"Why do we always meet when I'm asleep?"

"Well, we can meet at any time but, for now, you are new to splitting your consciousness so that you can be aware of multiple scenarios at the same time. The next step from where you are right now will be a kind of daydreaming, where you're aware of your Earthly surroundings at the same time as 'being' here."

"What must I do to obtain that ability?"

"Nothing, dear; it'll come naturally."

Loong rolls over onto his side.

"Why don't you rub my belly a little? I would certainly like that."

I am a little surprised; I thought Loong to be more mature that that.

"One never gets too old for a good belly-rub, and

it changes the energies to be more playful and less mental."

He is right and, as I start to rub his belly through the big layer of soft fur, I can clearly feel the playfulness and the joy he shares with me.

"I didn't think cats liked to get rubbed on their bellies."

"If they feel safe and are confident with the person, they quite enjoy it."

This playful moment drags me off my mental track, and I immerse myself in the happiness of sharing in a wonderful, timeless moment.

After this experience, Loong starts to talk about my work of collecting data for my book.

"There are many layers, facets and entanglements in the information that you are collecting. Some of it comes from a very narrow perspective. If presented as the truth, it may not be very accurate compared to a broader picture. For example, take the statement that dragons spew fire, as we talked about earlier. First, it's not fire, but 'energy', as you might say; bits of ideas and thought-forms. Second, dragons do not really exist; they are merely an expression of consciousness, conceived in a three-dimensional mind, partly derived from old memories."

"You've been following my journey. So how is it that the dragon symbol in the ancient Oracle Bone Script looks so much like a cat?"

"Highly-trained people with knowledge of writing were also the ones who had the knowledge of the other realms and were able to realise or sense the dragon souls in some cats. It would sound like the other way around, that the glyphs of a cat should look like a dragon, but since there really are no dragons, the cat was the animal that best represented us in the three-dimensional reality."

"You're not a cat either, you've told me, but consciousness, a soul."

"Different from cats, dragons come into existence by descending from higher planes. Like any soul, a dragon's soul is pure consciousness, and consciousness is the driving force in all creation. When a soul descends into a HUMAN life, it connects with a body already grown from two cells on the Earth plane. A soul that descends to a dragon's life creates its future body in a non-physical realm, and it then lowers the body's vibrations so that it appears in the physical dimension. It takes great skill and much training to maintain a physical body this way, but the advantage is that the body is 'clean'. Alternatively, it can take residence in an Earth-grown cat's body. If this cat already has a soul, there must be an agreement. Such a cat will usually have a karmic overlay from other lives, and hence it will not be 'clean'.

"In the old days, in the days of the dinosaurs, when souls were practising incarnation, dragons appeared as dinosaurs with feathers. The modern legend of what a dragon looks like derives from the findings of dinosaur bones in China, and as a karmic remembrance so, in a sense, the legend is true. No one BELIEVES in dragons these days, but some KNOW that they exist. It is not about appearance, but purpose. Dragons are not animals. Animals are in service to humanity, but evolve through their particular lines and are created through the planet. The animals that come closest to work with some of the same energies as the dragons are horses, deer and cattle. Not all of them, but a few. The energy those animals are working with could be called mother energy, a nurturing energy."

"I know that some dinosaurs had wings, but a heavy dragon with wings doesn't sound right, so why the wings?"

"The wings of a dragon are simply to show that the dragon is a spirit. It has nothing to do with flying. The wings of the dragons came to be in the same way that angels got their wings, and saints got their haloes above the head. The dragon appears as an animal surrounded by light, while an angel appears as a human surrounded by light. When dragons and angels present themselves to people in their light bodies, taking the same shape as an animal or a human, the outer part of the light body could be perceived as wings because it contains two elliptical bursts of light behind a central, denser, staff of light. Some human souls have a very condensed light body with one elliptic light burst, so only a small part of the burst can be seen above their heads, and can be perceived as a halo. The lower part hides below ground."

"How about dragons that are spewing fire?"

"The spewing of fire is to say that it is a powerful communicator. The fire is a communicative energy burst coming out of the area in front of the neck, not out of the mouth."

"How about the scales? You have fur, and you've talked about dinosaurs with feathers."

"I am consciousness, so I have no fur, but I know what you mean. Sometimes the dragon is depicted as a serpent with scales and front legs. The scales may provide some protection but will be a significant disadvantage in agility. A dragon in the shape of a cat relies on speed and agility. The saying that cats have nine lives comes from the dragons. Dragons reincarnate with full memory of previous lives, but they are, of course, not limited to nine lives on Earth; nor are humans, for that matter."

"Would you like some refreshments?"

I open my eyes and look at the stewardess, who is smiling at me.

"Sorry. Yes, still water, please."

"Get plenty," I hear Loong's voice from a distance. "Water is multi-dimensional, and will help you harmonise being in different realms at the same time."

"A large bottle, please."

I get the bottle and a plastic glass. Now I hear Loong's voice again.

"Haven't you experienced being sealed from the rain, and still being able to feel a drop of water on your skin?"

"Well, indeed I have! I only thought it was my imagination. How can that be?"

"Some part of the rain shifts from one 'dimension' to another, so the water drop you feel has shifted while falling. It doesn't fall through the shield, but merely appears on your skin from when it 'passes' into your Earthly reality."

I drink half of the water, and I feel refreshed and grounded in my body.

"I can hear you, but not see you; why is that?"

"The visual cortex is very powerful and connects you to your physical reality. You must realise that, when we meet, you have to EXPAND from your point of reality to mine; you don't MOVE or concentrate your thoughts to meet me. It must be a simple act, a choice, otherwise you'll concentrate and it'll then be an act of your mind, and your mind can't 'travel' outside its environment, which is 3D. Now close your eyes and let go of everything; thought and feelings."

Dragons and Knights

I close my eyes and take a deep breath, and slowly the noise in the cabin fades away. Now I can see the sunshine through my eyelashes. I open my imaginary eyes and am back with Loong in Elvendale. He changes the subject and poses me a question.

"How will you describe a knight - what he, or she, stands for?"

"Well, it must be something like pure of heart, high ethics, compassion, protector and defender of the weak, justice, merciful, not judgemental, honesty, courtesy, loyalty, generosity, keeps one's promises, prowess, courage, responsibility, hope."

"Good. One could say that the purpose of the dragons and Sidhe is to support these virtues in human consciousness. But, to do so, we must have a better connection, and that's where you and others come in. These virtues are personal, meaning that they GO OUT from the person, and are personal choices. We, dragons and Sidhe, see the virtues a little differently, since we look at their energy, and I'll specify them for you here in very short terms:

"Pure of heart: Do not go into lower emotions and actions that go against another.

"High Ethics: Doing the 'right' thing, even in stressful situations, which also takes courage. The right things are the highest human standards and well above any moral. The moral covers cultural laws, and a part of this is punishment.

"Compassion: One accepts other people's choices as theirs and gives them space to try them out. There is much more to this, but it must be left for some other time.

"Not judgemental: Like compassion.

"Protector and Defender of the weak: It happens in a non-forceful way, or else the energies will just fortify. Protection is a shield, while defending is speaking up or taking some non-offensive action.

"Justice: It happens in a non-forceful way, or else the energies will just fortify.

"Merciful: Show compassion and don't be revengeful.

"Generosity: Give 'wealth' and time, which is patience. Here you can add healing for free, as well as compassion.

"Honesty: Speak the truth, and always in a non-offensive way.

"Courtesy/kindness: Like compassion.

"Loyalty: Be loyal to yourself and trusting in your actions with others.

"Keep one's promises: Keeping promises is the same as being truthful.

"Prowess: Bless your body, and accept it as a part of you. Do light exercises.

"Courage: Show courage in YOUR actions and life. It has nothing to do with others.

"Responsibility: It's like the high ethics of doing the 'right' thing.

"Hope (and belief and trust): A purer and lighter form is optimism.

"Be a Standard: Be a model for the very best in humanity, by actually living to your highest potential. Teach by showing and not by preaching. Teaching by example, you might say.

"I just added the Standard. Most of these human virtues have the underlying energy of compassion - compassion for both self and others. Compassion is one of the many types of love there are, and we'll be talking about that later. Dragons also encourage people to be imaginative and curious, joyful, and expressive in art. You might say that we're fighting neglect, ignorance, chaos and disorder, but we're not fighting anything, we're deliberately doing the opposite. If you fight these things, your opponent will just throw more of these into the battle."

"Loong; to me, the knights who fought in the Holy Land and elsewhere did not seem especially compassionate, except for the cause."

"Many of the knights got those virtues distorted by the brutality of the common human consciousness. Their wish to do the right thing channelled into a brutal force. Just look at how the knights were fighting and killing for the 'good cause' of Christianity. It was a quite different consciousness in these years, and later the Knights Templar, their families and followers were persecuted and killed. The Christian church was becoming 'big business' in wealth and ruling power, and the Knights Templar were not buying into it but followed the earlier views from even before Christ. The crystal consciousness started to come in as early as 630 BC, to prepare for the coming of The Christ One. There is much more to this than just the figure, Jesus. He was just the one who was used to hang the hat on, so to speak; to bring the crystal consciousness 'down' into matter."

"What can you tell me about the legend of St George and the Dragon? Is it the killing of the physical, the flesh, so that the soul can rise to a purely divine existence?"

"In early Christian times you meet the knight killing the serpent or the dragon. The ignorance is killed to give space to a higher awareness. Another allegory is the Virgin Mary putting one foot on the serpent's neck. Many have interpreted it that way, but the message is just the same as we've been talking about: The physical AND the non-physical planes. That's why Mary does not KILL the snake. However, in the presentation, there is no equality between the two."

I enjoy sitting with Loong in the tall grass, sensing the whole scene at so many levels. I look up at the sky and see the V-shape of eleven swans passing high above our heads.

"Do you think it's safe if you take me for a short

flight?"

"Indeed; you can fly on your own, but I'll be delighted to take you on a short trip above the lands. Mount me as if I were a horse and grip on to my fur!"

I feel a little uncertain, but I decide to fully trust Loong when I sit behind the dragon's massive head.

"I'm ready!"

It is a gentle start, but soon we are high above the forest. Loong sets a course towards the city and, when we get closer, I see some kids waving at us from the access bridge to the city.

"I'm a real dragon-rider!"

"Indeed; you have become a Rider of the White Dragon!"

I wake up in my seat on the plane to Hong Kong, feeling a mild turbulence rocking the aircraft.

Back in Hong Kong

I am back in Hong Kong, primarily to find a way to be with Ju-long. I use the same hotel and am now at my grandparents'. It is in the afternoon; Grandpa is dozing in his armchair, and Grandma and I are sitting at the small, round, dining table.

"Did you have any success in Beijing and Shanghai, Luzi?"

"Yes, indeed! And definitely in ways I totally hadn't expected."

"Well, let me hear a little about it then."

"In Beijing, I visited Ling at the University. She and some of her students were about to leave for an archaeology dig. Luckily we had time enough to find similarities between Sidhe in Europe and Xian here. It was Josephine in Shanghai who connected Sidhe and dragons or more precisely, the Sidhe and the spirit of the soul of the dragon, which incarnates mostly as a cat."

I show Grandma the glyphs, but she has difficulty focusing on the subject.

"It's fascinating, but tell me how life is in Beijing and Shanghai, dear Luzi. We can prepare the dinner while you're telling me about it."

While cooking, I am telling a little of what I have seen on my trips. Ju-long texts me and suggests we meet at the beach, like last time, and I, of course, agreed to do so. I am dying to see him again.

Silly me; for thirty minutes I have tried to decide what to wear, as if it would matter much to Ju-long. As long as my outfit matches, it will be OK. It ends up being an above-knee, sleeveless, natural-white dress with print mostly in blue. I choose white shoes with some heel; not too much, since I am tall even without heels.

I feel that I have plenty of time, but end up by leaving the hotel just in time to meet Ju-long at the steps down to the beach.

Ju-long wears white sneakers, blue jeans and a T-shirt, matching my dress in colours. Interesting.

"You look adorable, Luzi."

I smile, but before I can say anything, we kiss… I have lost my breath, and it is not until Ju-long takes my hand and we start walking down the narrow stairs in slightly awkward positions that I get my speech back.

"It's wonderful to be with you again, and you look quite handsome, I must say."

"Thank you, Luzi."

We reach the stony beach and start to walk along the shoreline hand in hand. Ju-long seems intense and excited at the same time.

"There are some practical things to attend to, but I want to move to London as soon as possible so that we can be together."

"You must at least finish your courses before applying for a visa and a work permit. I think that a scholarship and an admission would give you your best chance of getting permission to stay in the UK."

"Luckily the last database course ends next month, so I'll get the certificate soon."

We talk more about the details, and we are both very excited about the whole thing of Ju-long moving to London and us being together. Ju-long walks me back to my hotel and we kiss for a long time in front of the hotel, neither of us wanting to leave. Some guests suddenly come out and break the magic, and we say goodnight.

Back in my room I am very excited and cannot find peace, even after a shower. At the same time, I feel relieved that we now have the larger lines laid out for our future. After talking to Ju-long, I believe that I can go back to London and continue my daily routines and get on with my book.

The next morning Ju-long calls me and asks me to meet him at the café across the street from the library. I arrive at nine and find him waiting for me. He is looking quite bad, in a kind of shock, and has probably not slept last night. We sit down outside.

"I can't see how I can move from my mother and grandparents. Yesterday evening, after meeting you, I was sitting observing these three people. It became apparent to me that my grandparents are getting old and are unable to fully care for themselves, and Mother is a frail woman, not able to carry the burden of providing both money and care for them by herself."

"I would like to meet your family; not that I doubt your judgement or decision, but they're a part of you."

"I would prefer that you visit only as the former classmate whom I met at the library. I don't want them to feel guilty in any way."

Ju-long has to go back to work, and I start to walk slowly around in the area, feeling dizzy and quite beside myself. The surroundings seem blurred, and the sounds are like listening through a pillow. My senses are numb. I realise that visiting my grandparents today is not an option, so I call them, get Grandmother on the phone and say that I do not feel very well and will go to sleep early.

After a dinner of fruits, I meet Ju-long outside the entrance to the block where he lives with his family. A quick kiss and we walk upstairs to the flat. Ju-long walks in first and then I am introduced to first his grandparents and then his mother. His mother is now a fragile woman, without the strength she had in the earlier days when Ju-long and I were kids. Her name is Ting. I remember his grandparents as always smiling and loving people, but now the smiles are gone except for the moment we say hello. I know them only as Mr and Mrs Lin.

I am standing in a small hall lit by a sleepy bulb, casting its yellow light on everything, giving it the same yellow colour. From the hall there are doors to the bathroom and a bedroom. Straight ahead I can see the living room. The feeling of this place is very different from my grandparents'. The energy is low, and I feel a kind of sadness and hopelessness. We walk into the living room and here I must have some fresh air.

"Could you please open a window? I don't feel quite well, Ju-long."

"Yes, of course; we must just be careful that no one gets caught in a draught, Luzi."

Overprotective? Some fresh air might do us all some good.

The kitchen is part of the living room, and at the far end there is a door to what I suppose must be another bedroom.

"This is my corner!"

Ju-long points at the far corner next to the bedroom door. Here there is a small table and a cabinet with his things and, probably, his sleeping mattress. I see no computer, so he must use those at the library. His corner; like a dog has its corner with a basket and a blanket. Why did I get that thought?

The decorations are in general nostalgic, as if they want to hold tight to some elusive happiness from the past, from the good old days. Added to this, everything seems worn out; some things have been repaired or have missing parts, and are really in need of replacement. There are broken woodwork, worn-out furniture covers and old blankets. The smoke from candles and incense is on everything.

It will be a short visit. I must get out as quickly as I can without being impolite. We talk about the past, and I tell about my life in London. To fill the gaps of silence, I tell about my trips, first with my family in my younger years and then the later trips without my family.

I am back on the street, and it has started to rain. Ju-long is with me.

"Wait here! I'll get an umbrella and walk you to the hotel!"

"Please, Ju-long, I would like to walk alone and try to clear my thoughts and feelings. I really need to."

"I'm sorry for causing you all this pain, Luzi. I hope we can meet tomorrow."

"Yes, we'll meet tomorrow, but I have to go back to London in a day or two. There are work and courses I have to attend to."

Ju-long returns with an old umbrella and, after a quick kiss, I am on my way back to the hotel at a fast pace. Now it starts to rain heavily as if all tears from Heaven must fall on me tonight.

I must agree that Ju-long's mother and grandparents could not carry on without Ju-long or some kind of help, at least. I was devastated when the truth fully got a grip on me. It was as if I were just falling and falling into an infinite black hole of despair and disbelief. To move to Hong Kong seems to be my only option, but then what about my beloved jobs and classes at the university, my flat, and my friends? Must I give up all this? It is my whole life!

Shortly after I have left Ju-long the umbrella breaks, so I throw it in a litter bin. Soaking wet, I return to the hotel. Back in my room I take a hot shower, trying to wash away all that the heavy rain could not, but in vain. Lying on my back in bed, I can feel that I will doze off in seconds.

First, it's dark. Then I start to sink, like into a big, black pillow. After that it brightens, and I open my eyes, lying in the same spot as I did the first time I came to Elvendale. The smells are back, and so are all the sounds; even the choir is there. I hear a deep snort and raise myself up on my elbow. How good it is once again to be with Loong. I do not feel exhausted any longer.

"You think that the connection between Ju-long and you goes back to your childhood, but it goes further back in history, into other lives. You've been sisters with very close relations and, before that, a man and a woman, who could not have each other because the families demanded it be otherwise. In the life as sisters, you had an almost symbiotic relationship, even though you weren't twins."

"How can previous lives have an influence on the current one?"

"You can say that what has happened in another life is recorded, and reminiscences are in the consciousness of humanity. If some issues have not been relieved, they'll tie up to the present life. This time, the energies of the former lives play out in this life as 'desperately want to be together' and 'families don't allow'. It's not Ju-long's family that denies you being together, but the energy plays out in a way that it seems that his family needs him, and he has to withdraw from you."

"What can we - I mean he and I - do to change this terrible situation?"

"What will happen if Ju-long releases himself from those energies and gives the responsibility for his mother and his grandparents back to them? Well, new energies or possibilities will come in and he will be able to choose from them, no longer bound by the old belief system of sacrificing oneself. Likewise, it'll take a resolving of your relations, in the plural, to make the way for new possibilities for you and Ju-long."

"So this situation is not real, in a sense, since something mingles with it; but I've visited him and his family, and it seems quite real to me!"

"The illusion comes in before Ju-long 'thinks' or 'feels' that he MUST take responsibility. What would have happened if he was not there for some reason? The situation would simply have played out differently. It had to. Maybe his mother would still be stuck with her parents because she, too, thinks that she is responsible for them; but again, there are many possibilities. And if she had not been around, would her parents have made different choices, now that they didn't have to play this game of responsibility?"

"But if Ju-long leaves them, his mother may be working herself to death to support her parents!"

"Only if she chooses to, or, better said, if THEY choose it. She can make a conscious choice to cut the karmic bond and old beliefs, and both she and her parents may have far better lives than they have at the moment."

"But Loong, parents MUST take responsibility for their children."

"Yes, yes, that is built into most animals as part of nature, but they must not provide for their young all their lives! THAT is unnatural, it really is."

"So you are saying that Ju-long isn't responsible for his mother and grandparents!"

"It depends on what you put into the meaning of responsibility, but yes, that's what I'm saying. If someone needs help, the whole of society has to be built in such a way, whether you need the plumbing fixed, or been taken care of your health. It's why you have so many specialised jobs. It is not up to each single child or parent to take this responsibility."

"I know that I cannot talk to Ju-long about karmic bonds and past lives. Even IF I can persuade him to leave his family, he can still blame me if his mother or grandparents do not get themselves out of the karmic wheel, and live the rest of their lives in misery."

"Yes, but his love for you might be the catalyst that forces him to break free. It might even create a chain reaction that influences the rest of the family for the better."

"But I have to move to Hong Kong so that I can be with Ju-long!"

"Or maybe you, living in London, may create the pull that is needed for Ju-long to get free. It could be part of the set-up for a solution."

"It would be as if I were forcing him to leave his family in Hong Kong and come to me."

"Well, in a way, it's exactly what you are doing, but it's still up to Ju-long to make the decision. You can never decide for him; it's a personal choice."

The next morning, it is evident to me that I must entangle myself in the web of Ju-long and his family. I must hope and believe that our love will be strong enough to break that 'spell' for the benefit of all. The next flight to the UK is very early the next morning, which I tell Ju-long and my grandparents. I spend my time with my grandparents. I always have the feeling that I may not see them again, so I am always in a particular mood at these hours of my visit.

In the afternoon, I meet Ju-long outside the library at five pm to say goodbye. Because of the early flight tomorrow morning, this is the time to make the terrible break until we will meet again, hopefully not so far in the future.

"Dear Ju-long, I'm not drawing away from you, but a lot is going on in my thoughts and feelings. It's mostly about us, but also about my grandparents, and I fear this may be the last time I will see them. With all these feelings whirling around, I turn inside to find a calm place in myself."

"I feel the same way leaving my family, especially my mother, and I may not see my grandparents again, either. And all the new things I must face when I move to London. Yes, even HOW to arrange all of it."

After this we stand for a long time, mostly in silence, just holding each other tight, before I finally leave and go back to my grandparents.

We are spending the rest of the day mostly as we used to do but, after the short walk to the top of the stairs leading down to the beach and back, we say our goodbyes. We are standing outside their block, and I give them both a long hug.

"It was so nice to see you both, and I hope we will see each other real soon."

Grandpa is moved and holds me in his arms for a long time.

"You're always welcome, Luzi. Have a safe journey

tomorrow and say hello to Carl, Ya and Anna."

Grandma is equally moved and, after a long hug, she looks me in the eyes and assures me that everything will work out fine.

"Dear, dear, Luzi, these have been some really eventful days, but we're sure that everything will turn out for the best. Remember that massive changes may take some time to fall into place."

My eyes are full of tears as I walk the short way to the hotel. I feel tired and awake at the same time but, when I pull the sheets over me, I almost instantly slip into a deep sleep.

I can feel Josela's kind and loving presence, but we are not in Elvendale. It is dark, but it is not scary, it is simply just the absence of light. After a few moments, she speaks to me.

"I have promised you we would talk about angelic families. 'Angel' is just a popular term, as is the term 'soul', for that matter. Let's just say that offspring of the creative consciousness had left home to explore their new-found sovereignty and played with energy created at the same time as they got their sovereignty. At some point, they gathered in groups of 'like mind' and, later, the 'thought' came out that they might be incomplete or less than their parents and should return home to gain completeness. At the same time, this thought of being less gave the impression that energy was limited. Now they had to gather as much energy as they could, even steal it from others, and the battles began."

"So, this was the first Star Wars!?"

"Well, not in the way you think. We were not physical at that time. The battles for energy continued and energy became more and more stuck, and things started to slow down. All came almost to a standstill and, to find a solution, a council emerged. Here it was decided to create a physical environment; this is slow in comparison to consciousness, which acts in an instant. Just think how slowly your brain works."

"Yes, the brain is not only slow, but it works only in a three-dimensional environment."

"And we were looking for exactly that. This way it was easier to experience what was really going on in our lives. We could watch it all in slow motion."

I can feel some disturbance, and I start to fade away from Josela.

"What is happening?"

"You're feeling some of the unrest and fear from the whole situation, especially the battles. Let's close for now, and I'll promise to continue when things have calmed down for you."

She gives me a warm hug and, shortly after, I wake up with a feeling of unrest and alertness. Luckily I can fall asleep again, but only to wake up to the sound of my alarm. After the checkout at the hotel, I take a taxi all the way to the airport. It is 40 km, or 25 miles, and the most convenient method to get there, especially so early in the morning when I am not quite awake.

While on the plane to London, Josela returns to complete her story about the angels.

"As the physical stage was set, one representative from each family was selected to join the first wave of explorers in the dense environment. First, we had to train to get used to this life, so we started to swim with the whales as conscious passengers, not incarnated. Later came the Lemuria period."

"So, we are still trying to find out how to get back?"

"Well, not really. At some point we got lost in the physical environment and reincarnation, but some 'woke up' and became aware of what was really going on. It's what you call 'ascension' or 'enlightenment'."

"So, the masters are trying to tell the rest of us what is really going on?"

"YES! It's so simple; but, as humans are so stuck in their earthly lives, even simple things can be difficult."

After this talk, I am eager to pursue the masters' teachings in a new light, although it could not be a part of my current book. Before I land at Heathrow, I realise that the masters use two approaches to wake people up. One is to teach them how to reach enlightenment, and the other is to give them knowledge about what is really going on.

London

In the evening I call my parents, as it has been some time since we have talked. I tell them about my book and, of course, about my trips to various places in China. I tell them about my meeting with Ju-long, as it fills my thoughts and feelings most of the day. Mum tries to encourage me.

"As you know, love is a mighty motivator. I'm sure you'll pull in the solutions."

Now Dad comes up with something that might be exactly the right solution.

"Dear Luzi, I think we can solve this. You see, I've invested quite a bit in social care, health care and elderly care in China, and not only in Hong Kong. We have a privately-driven institution in Hong Kong and, if the conditions of Ju-long's grandparents can pass the criteria, and I add my recommendations, we'll find a way."

"It'll help us, and take the heat off the situation."

"We have some great people in Hong Kong. They know the social laws in depth and have many connections in the community. Don't worry; I'll look into it as soon as I can get hold of someone in Hong Kong, and I'll send some emails right away."

Mum and I continue talking for a while, and I get the latest updates on her busy life.

I cannot wait to bring the good news to Ju-long. I

do not want to text or email him, so I must wait for him to get to work and I will call him there. I set my alarm clock for two am so that I can call Ju-long at the library at ten o'clock Hong Kong time.

When the alarm clock rings, I need some time to come to the surface. I turn on the light, pee, and drink a glass of water. I call the library in Hong Kong and have Ju-long's voice in my ear after a small wait.

"Hi Luzi, I've been desperate to hear from you! How are you?"

"I'm much calmer than the last time we spoke. I have been talking to Dad about China and Hong Kong, where people get older having fewer young people to care and pay for them. He told me that he had invested quite a bit in elderly care facilities of different kinds, especially in Hong Kong. I didn't know that. He promised to look into it and contact me about the immediate result."

"Yes, I remember your dad, Carl…"

"Your grandparents aren't getting younger, and you can't live the rest of your life in the hope that things will become better. Dad is pretty sure that he can help in some way."

"I'll not talk about it at home because I won't give them false hopes."

"But maybe hope for a brighter future is all it takes to start the process of breaking out of this circle of despair."

"You may be right, Luzi. Without hope, nothing will change for the better."

"Yes, without hope and, even more, a will to change things, you only have the illusion that luck will bring the changes that you need."

Our optimism is back, and we talk once again about Ju-long's opportunities for moving to London. Then we end the conversation. He has to go back to work, and I must leave to get to the university. I have different things to attend to here, but later I will spend the rest of the day at the library.

Senate House Library is the central library of the University of London, and the home library for the School of Advanced Study. It is early in the afternoon, and I have just left the library and am walking down the stairs outside. Just opposite the library, I see the rear of the British Museum. I have seen it hundreds of times, but today I feel a strange urge to pay the Museum a visit. I always use the library or the online libraries, as the Internet but, at this moment, I realise that a museum is just a different kind of library. You could say that it is a library of physical things, where the library only holds information about physical things and, of course, so much other stuff as well.

I enter the museum and go straight to the overview map. I stand in front of the map for a while, hoping that it will tell me where to find something of importance. Then my eyes stop at the label: "Room 33c, Dragon tiles." From the map, it seems to be quite a small room but, in this case, size probably does not matter. I walk through the grand entrance hall with the columns on each side and find the dragon tiles. I look closely to see if there are any details to link cats and dragons, or other clues I can use in my book. Sadly, I can see nothing of interest. Disappointed, I decide to leave the Museum, since the urge to enter here may not have been real. On my way out, I walk over to the columns on the right to follow the row to the exit. Again I feel an urge and look around.

Hmm; what is going on with me today? I feel sensitive and alert, but I cannot see any signs.

That is not entirely accurate. There is ONE sign saying: "Room 4, Egyptian sculptures." Since this is the ONLY sign, I walk into Room 4. The first thing that catches my eye is a statue of a sitting cat, cast in some metal. "The Gayer-Anderson cat," the label says, "Named after its donor."

The short text next to the sculpture tells me that the life-size cat is cast in bronze. On its head it has the relief of a scarab beetle, around the neck a good-luck charm with "The Eye of Horus," and on the chest a winged scarab holding the Sun.

There are no leads to dragons, except maybe the wings on the scarab, but I will investigate further when I return to my study.

Back in my study I find out that a lot of sculptures look very similar to this one, even the small ones you buy as souvenirs.

Loong comes through with a comment on that.

"You'll see that most of the Egyptian art and symbols are depicted very similarly, even throughout several periods. It should tell you that they carry archetypical information as well as historical and practical meanings."

As I investigate further about Egyptian cats, I find out that Bast is the goddess of cats. She has the attributes of protection, joy, dance, music and love - the same attributes as Hathor, usually depicted with cow-horns on the top of her head, not growing out from her head, and the solar disc between the horns. Many see Bast as the predecessor of Sekhmet, the lion goddess, who has the head of a lion and a solar disc on the top of her head. The solar disc has a snake as well.

Wow, the exact attributes as my experiences with the Sidhe!

Bast's father is Ra, the Sun, and her mother is Isis. Ra is the light-giver, and Isis is the ideal mother and the patroness of nature and magic.

More symbols from the Sidhe realm!

In its essence, the scarab symbolises the circle of life and life on Earth itself. As it rolls a ball of dung, hence also called dung beetle, it also rolls the Sun across the sky, and brings it back after the night. Light and dark, life and death - a repeating cycle, a spiral. In the cycle, reincarnation plays a vital role.

Horus is the god of the Sun, and therefore also the son of the Sun; son of Ra. As he is also the son of Isis, he is a brother to Bast. In different cults there were different relationships between them, but it does not change the fact that there was, and is, a close connection. The imposed human relationships are just to make it easier for people to relate to the archetypes.

We have the masculine and the feminine aspects. The masculine Sun brings life from 'above' and the feminine nature provides the womb, the dark, the night, and the nourishment from the Earth.

So the symbols, as well as the cat figure itself, bring many aspects forth.

The scarab on the head shows that the intellect, the mind, is part of the Earth or the three-dimensional world, while life itself, the soul, the consciousness, is placed in the heart area - another symbolic meaning. The scarab on the chest of the statue has the wings of Isis and carries the Sun in its front legs. The wings symbolise the soul, the eternal life, not bound to the physical life on Earth. The Sun is the creative force and, as mentioned before, the scarab is Earthly life.

Again, the winged scarab shows that there is more to life (the scarab) than the physical, namely the soul (the wings).

After all this I realise that I AM guided by Sidhe and Loong to bring forth these truths. I usually see myself as a very intellectual person but, in this case, I have a very intuitive connection to something much deeper and more essential to life.

Now I have more material for my book, demanding

a lot of research according to the Egyptian angle.

Egypt

It has been a busy day, so I have not had the time to check my personal email account. Now, back in my lovely flat, I turn on my computer and prepare some fruit and a jug of water. There is a message from Dad, and my heart starts to beat faster.

"Dear Luzi, the Hong Kong people have sent a form to Ju-long to get the details, and they're pulling some strings as well. I'll return with more news as soon as I have any. Mum and I are making the final preparations for a two-week trip to Egypt… Mum has just shown up and asks if you might have time to spend some days with us in Egypt. We're well and looking forward to this trip. Kisses, Mum & Dad."

Egypt! Synchronicity? I check my calendar. I can take a few days off, or maybe a week if I can shift things around a little.

There is an email from Ju-long as well.

"Dear, lovely Luzi, we've got a form from the HK Care Foundation, and I've talked with a man on the phone as well. They want a lot of details, so it was nice to have him to assist me with the form. Mum and my grandparents are sceptical and uncertain about all this, but someone from the Foundation will come and talk to us this evening. At this point we don't know how they can support us. I've briefly mentioned to my family the possibility of moving to London. I miss you a whole lot. Kisses and hugs, Ju-long."

I answer Ju-long right away.

"My dear Ju-long, I miss you too. Lovely to hear that the Foundation is working so fast, and I hope you'll get a more concrete answer soon. Mum and Dad are going to Egypt for two weeks, and as I have found some leads to Egyptian cats in my book. I might be joining them for a couple of days. Hope to hear more good news from you soon. Kisses, Luzi."

Then a short answer to Mum and Dad.

"Hi! Sounds great about a trip to Egypt. Please let me have some dates and I'll see how I can rear-range my calendar. Today I found some clues for my book, and guess what? It's about prehistoric Egyptian cats! I've got a message from Ju-long: the Foundation is working fast; they have filled out a form, and they are visiting the family tonight! Thanks, Dad! I'm Looking forward to being with you in Egypt. Love, Luzi."

The preparations for the trip to Egypt are easy. Everything seems to work in my favour and, before long, I am on a plane to Egypt and, without doubt, to new discoveries proven by the synchronicity of it all.

I have arrived at Cairo International Airport just before midnight, after a five-hour flight. I take the shuttle to the national terminal and wait here for the connection to Luxor at five a.m. Luckily, I had some sleep on the plane from London, and an e-book keeps me company until the security opens, with some delay.

The small plane lands in Luxor after a one-hour flight, and I take a taxi to the Sonesta St George Hotel on Corniche El Nile Street, where my parents are staying. We share an early breakfast, and then I sleep for a few hours in my room.

In the afternoon I explore the hotel, and one of the first places I find is a small perfume shop in the hall next to the elevator. Here a man, Esmail, sells me a perfume which, when I smell it the first time, moves me so much that tears run down my cheeks. It must have touched some hidden experiences from another time; probably in Egypt. It is wonderful to be with my parents this way, being at exotic places in completely joy and awe, like in my younger days. After sunset, we take a walk in the neighbourhood of the hotel to experience the place away from the scorching heat of the sun during the day. It hurts me to see the small, skinny horses pulling the taxi carriages. I feel the owners do not see the horse as a living being, but more as a tool for income. It is a proof of low consciousness, and we choose not to use any of them.

The next morning we board the Nile cruiser, Movenpick Royal Lily, which is a five-star hotel ship. Royal Lily would take us up and down the Nile, docking at specific places along the river to let us attend specially arranged tours.

I will not tell you about all the visits, but only an extraordinary experience, since it brings another thread to the Sidhe/Chinese connection.

In Luxor, we visit the Karnak temple. A small temple for Sekhmet lies way behind the large Karnak temple complex. Close by, on a bridge, guards armed with machine-guns are on patrol. In a small room there is a black or dark grey statue of Sekhmet, the lion goddess. I feel quite devout. Sekhmet says to me, "Why are you being so serious? Let's dance." And so we did; a swirling dance in a big room; around and around, in great joy. Outside again in the sunshine, standing by some large column sections, Imhotep appears on the scene.

"You can't split the consciousness up into different gods with predefined attributes; yes, you met Sekhmet, but you were dancing with Sekhmet, Bast, Hathor and Isis… well, and all the rest of us. Her primary attribute, strength, has been, and still is, greatly misunderstood. It has nothing to do with power, which is usually an ego thing used to manipulate and to take control over others. Her strength tells you that you must stand in your own light, never being in someone else's shadow. That is why you felt the love and the joy during the dance; the joy of freedom from any suppression."

You may ask, dear reader, how I know I am communicating with Imhotep. It is simply the name with which this consciousness presented itself when it first touched me, and I felt the truth and the love that it was indeed a consciousness I had known in the past.

"I'm sure that you know that like me, whom you've known as Imhotep in another life, Sekhmet can connect with you anytime and anywhere, if you're open to it. The statue was just the conductor for your meeting, but you might find it interesting that, if you draw a line from the Luxor Temple through the causeway with the rams, you'll hit the small temple with the statue of Sekhmet."

I immediately feel a deep connection to Imhotep and realise that we have known each other in other lives, not only in the one I have known him under that name.

"Actually, you've known me with the name Imhotep in some lifetimes here in Egypt. Stories say that I became very old; well I did, but I also replaced the body to stay in these parts for an extended period. I felt that I could not die and leave the 'space' it would create to power-hungry individuals."

I feel that I am in an expanded reality, both standing here in the morning sun with ruins all around me and, at the same time, deeply connected to this entity in what feels a very natural way.

"Why have I never experienced this before - I mean, connecting in this way?"

"There have been connections, a lot of them, but you have never actually listened to the voices. That's OK, because you've been quite good at sensing the feelings we use to communicate with you. Feelings, not emotions, are a much better way of communication."

"Oh, like when I felt drawn to the museum, back in London?!"

"Yes, and to come back to the connections you're seeking. It's all connected. The symbol or glyph that is known as The Eye of Horus pre-dates the Egyptian culture and was found in the secret knowledge in Atlantis. When I and some others came to Egypt, we brought these secrets with us. There were only primitive humans living here at that time, so, of course, we could only teach them very basic stuff, usually brought to them in parables. By different means, over time, we were able to enhance the original inhabitants to some degree. Later on the people degraded like the rest of humanity, due to a decrease in consciousness caused by their focus on the material world. The Egyptian word for The Eye of Horus is, by the way, 'Wedjat', who is one of the earliest deities. As I said before, this symbol is ancient, and it may interest you to know that a similar symbol or symbols can be found in the ancient Chinese glyphs if you take your time to browse through them."

This is what I found out later:

The Eye of Horus in traditional Egyptian style.

*"To see" in Chinese Oracle Bone character
(2000-1027 BC, Xia & Shang dynasties).*

*"To see" in traditional Chinese (Radical 147)
(206 BC - now). In classical Chinese, it means "appear".*

"Appear" also means to come into existence. Everything that comes into existence manifests through consciousness. The concept of 'the centre of all things' is very old!

I found this eye glyph below as an example of writing done on tortoise shells from the Peiligang culture in China from around 7000-5700 BC. It even has the two 'lines' below the eye! How can this NOT be evidence of connections over huge distances and time? I simply cannot believe that these signs have been carried on food over vast distances and remembered through millennia; it must have been common conscious knowledge.

A sign used around 7000 BC at Jiahu, Henan Province, China. Carbon-dated to 6500-6200 BC.

I wander off by myself so as not to be distracted in conversation with my parents. We have a set time to meet at the entrance, so there is no problem. At

one time I am completely alone in a large court-
yard, standing in the warm sun just sensing the
place.

"Pick up the stone you see there."

I look down and see a stone which is lighting up
because the sun is shining through it. I pick it up
and, when I look more closely, I see it has a crystal
shape, but with worn-out points. It looks almost as
if two square-based pyramids were put together
bottom to bottom, with one peak pointing up and
the other pointing down. It is called an octahedron
because of its eight sides.

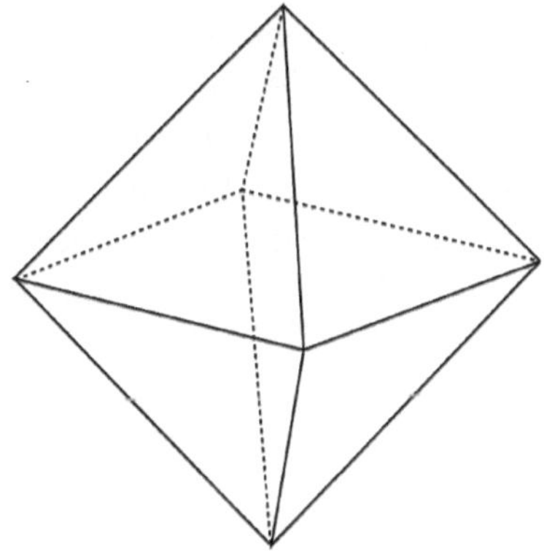

This sketch shows the octahedron.

"Oh, thanks. Now I can carry some of the light
from Egypt back with me."

I look at the small crystal for a while; then I put it in
my pocket. I have felt a growing need coming up,

and I think to myself,

"Now I can really use a bathroom."

"Just continue the way you are facing."

Well, there does not look to be anything in that direction, but I will try it anyway. I pass through an opening in a wall and, not far from me to the left there is a small building hidden half below ground and behind some trees. There is a wooden sign saying "WC".

"Thanks!"

"You're welcome!"

It proves to me that consciousness is outside of time and space, and that death is an illusion. I can have a conversation with a long-dead Egyptian about a trivial subject like finding a bathroom! There is nothing devout about the connection; it is just a meeting of equal ranking, soul to soul.

Lemuria and Atlantis

I am back at the Royal Lily in my cabin and have just had a refreshing shower. I am now lying on the bed waiting for dinner to be served, thinking of what has happened during the day. I decide to pose a question to Imhotep.

"Now that I have the opportunity, I'll ask you about the building technique of the pyramids. How were these huge stones lifted into place?"

"The pyramids are built like gigantic crystals, like those used in Atlantis. Some in the shape of the crystal you have just found, an octahedron. The short answer to the question about the heavy lifting is that it was done with consciousness, but that's not an answer you can use, so I'll elaborate. In what you know as Atlantis, we used crystals to store energy and 'programs' for many different tasks. Electrical energy was not prevalent at that time. One of those 'programs' or 'codes' could significantly reduce gravity, and was controlled by consciousness; not thought or mind, but consciousness. We brought one of those crystals with us when we came to Egypt. It was actually the one that Moses took with him when he left Egypt with his people. That was the reason why the Pharaoh went after the Jews after he had allowed them to leave Egypt. With this crystal, they could part the waters as well."

"So when Atlantis sank into the ocean, you went to Egypt?"

"Oh, Atlantis didn't sink into the ocean. After the last Ice Age, the water level rose and covered some of the shores and the scientific centre, Tian, which gives rise to the story of the Bermuda Triangle. The myth about the sinking of Atlantis derives from Lemuria, the first era of incarnation on this planet, when most of the lands, with their rejuvenation centre, sank within a hundred-year period because the magma bubble under it contracted so only the Hawaiian Islands remained above sea level. When people are trying to sense into the Atlantis period, they are overburdened by the previous history and the immense fear that the sinking of the land produced. One of the stepping-stones for the Lemurians was Easter Island, which they reached in canoes after sensing in which direction they should sail to find safe land. Many did not reach land, though."

"Well, what really happened to Atlantis?"

"That's a very sad story indeed! The old Atlantis still exists, but in a non-physical realm, outside the three-dimensional world, as you might say. This non-physical Atlantis was created, first as an experiment and later as a refuge, when things got tough due to a power-hungry leader named Azuru Timu and his followers. Timu was a title, and means 'leader', or 'the one who takes care of the people.' Azuru means 'blue', referring to his bluish skin. Eventually Azuru Timu died, after having lived for 550 years by feeding on other people's life energy.

"The structure of Atlantis had fallen apart during the ruling of Azuru Timu, and at that time the common human consciousness was quite low. It affected the Earth, causing extreme weather conditions, volcano eruptions and earthquakes. The volcano eruptions and, to a degree, earthquakes added to the situation and made the weather even more extreme, with lower temperatures and sandstorms covering out the sunlight. When the conditions on the surface of the Earth became intolerable, people moved underground into large cave-cities for hundreds of years. Crystals, from the days of Earth's creation, provided the people with energy to sustain life in the caves. All this caused a major setback to human life in general, and much knowledge vanished from the general population."

"When were the Lemuria and Atlantis eras?"

"You must know that time isn't linear, and scientists aren't taking that into consideration when calculating history. You can say that Lemuria started roughly five hundred million years ago and Atlantis about five hundred thousand years ago, if we see the great exodus from Lemuria as the start of it."

"If Atlantis hasn't sunk into the ocean, then where is it?"

"Well, it is all over the Earth, but the centre was Mexico City, so you could say that it's the Americas. There were places now submerged in the Pacific Ocean off the coast, and areas now in the Atlantic Ocean off the coast of Cuba. The city of Tien, with its temples and schools, lies here."

"How can time not be linear? If I look at my watch, time progresses second by second."

"The less conscious humans are, the slower time passes through this consciousness or, more correctly, the fewer events happen. Since consciousness fluctuates, the same does time. You have actually experienced this yourself. You can feel that an event happens slowly or quickly; it depends on how much awareness you put into the event. From our perspective, not being physical, we look at history as events passing through consciousness. To us it is not days ticking away, controlled by your clocks. When you ask me for a specific year, I have to pick a reference point and calculate the years back to the event in question. If you ask another one you may get a different year, depending on the reference point and the weight of the fluctuating consciousness. The best way for you to measure consciousness 'levels' is to look at inventions and arts. The more inventions and art an epoch produces, the higher the consciousness is."

"If Atlantis was or is America, are the native Indians then ancestors of the Atlantians?"

"You can say that most of the human population on Earth today are the ancestors of the Atlantians. At the later time of the Atlantis era, the human body was being altered and conformed into seven races - four ordinary races and three ruling races. The intelligence was improved as well. The three ruling races have vanished due to inter-breeding because they wanted to stay pure. In Lemuria we incarnate in all kinds of bodies, tiny ones and some very large; some look like animals and others like humanoids. The Atlantians chose Homo Sapiens for the conformity."

126

"So the 'Out of Africa' theory just won't connect to the modern human, because of the alterations during the Atlantis era?"

"Well since life and, therefore, also humanoids, evolved all over the globe, that theory does not fit anyway. It's just like inventions; they pop up in several places all over the globe. It's in the consciousness of humanity."

"Does this fit with Plato's description that he got from Egypt?"

"Well, yes. The story talked about the land where the city, Tien, with its temples and schools, was situated east of nowadays Cuba, as I said before. To the west of Atlantis, there was a grand land that truly could be called a continent. Of course, this is America. The place that the Egyptians were talking to Plato about was only the area with the temples, where skilled people conducted wide variations of experiments. There were no religious beliefs at that time."

"How were the Atlantians able to alter their bodies?"

"They altered the DNA using crystals; they were used partly as magnetic tweezers, working directly on a chromosome."

"How was that even possible!?"

"As I have told you before, consciousness was used to work with the crystals, and they KNEW what they were doing. Today you use only mechanics, chemicals, and markers to manipulate genes. There is no magic in this; humanity has simply forgotten to be conscious because of the focus on the physical world. What you see and feel is real. Today it has to be tangible to be of any use. It was not that difficult since all mammals have very similar DNA, with only slight differences."

"At least some of them had to be very smart people to pull this off."

"Oh no; they just have to KNOW that it can be done and know where to look in the genome. It is not enough to BELIEVE it because someone says that it is so. Take the Lemurians; they were not intelligent at all, and still they KNEW how the universe works; they knew everything about the solar system and the galaxies. They had universal knowledge. As they had the knowledge of 'the outside', so they had the knowledge of 'the inside'."

"Why don't we have that knowledge today?"

"It's partially because the focus has changed to be about surviving and accumulating wealth, love and power, and partially because of blockages placed in and around the brain in the late Atlantian era, when the unification took a wrong turn and became controlling and manipulating. Select groups of people received headbands as a prestige token but they were, in fact, designed to control them. These headbands could both limit and enhance. Take the king's crown, for example."

"We don't usually wear headbands today, and our brains have not altered, so what is wrong?"

"The alterations have, over millennia, gone into the mass consciousness, and now everyone is affected. You can remove these blockages, though, through a conscious choice."

"The mass consciousness is the consciousness of all humans, right?"

"Yes; it's an artificial consciousness derived from human experiences building up through millennia. It has taken a 'life' on its own. Some call it 'The Little God', because it manipulates and draws strength from humanity, like a vengeful god that expects worship and admiration - a true picture of the human ego."

"How could all the ancient knowledge, that you talked about before, disappear?"

"As people became more and more power-hungry, the wise ones in the communities hid the knowledge over time, so it became secret knowledge. Some of these secrets had to be hidden in plain sight, as you say, so the ones who were conscious enough to handle it could find it. Good examples are the stories of the Egyptian gods; they are instructions for manipulating the genes. That's why they have such strange relationships and their behaviour is quite odd. Just look at the stories around Horus, and the eye of Horus. You must know that is was not meant to be hidden from people in general; it was hidden to protect the general population from being abused by those in power."

The Grand Exodus from Lemuria

Imhotep tells more about Atlantis and Lemuria.

"Hawaii was the centre of Lemuria since it was here the Temple of Rejuvenation was, in the mountain, close to the top. It was one large island before it sank. Most Lemurines were settled, with no desire for leaving their lands. They were content with living off the land and attending to working the earth. At some point some of them decided to seek new lands, for different reasons. They didn't want to go west, since Asia was part of the Lemurian world. The easiest way off Hawaii was to follow the sea currents north and then north-east to the Americas in the later months of the year. The wind phenomena, El Niño and La Niña, also played their part. Here they found new places to live. They called it Alt - what you know as Atlantis."

I have dug a little into genetics to see if I could learn something that would support the expansion from Lemuria to Atlantis. The most interesting studies I found were some results showing that humans populated the Americas BEFORE the most accepted invasions through Beringia, which is the 'land bridge' between Siberia and Alaska, in waves starting 19,000 years BP (before present day); this is called the short chronology theory. The long chronology theory states that invasions started 21,000 to 40,000 years BP, followed by much later invasions.

ALL Amerindians (Native Americans) have common genes that do not include the Athabaskans and Inuits (from Beringia and Siberia). This indicates that the introduction of these genes happened later, AFTER America got a homogeneous population. A further indication of this is that Lakota-Sioux Amerindians who inhabit the Northern United States are not related to Asians and West Siberians, but to Meso (middle) and South Americans. Some new, extended four loci haplotypes (genealogical term) have been found only in Amerindian and Aleut (a portion of the Alaska Peninsula) specific groups and in no other Amerindian or world populations. I have placed a link on this at the end of the book under 'sources'.

The global sea levels have risen over 120 metres, or 390 feet, since the end of the last glacial period about 21,000 years ago. This means that added to the volcanoes, earthquakes and extreme weathers changing the face of the planet, so has the rising sea level, and covering a large number of the scars from the violent period, where the remaining Atlantians searched refuge below ground.

Today there is much more water that covers land, so it is no wonder that we now and then find human-made constructions under the sea.

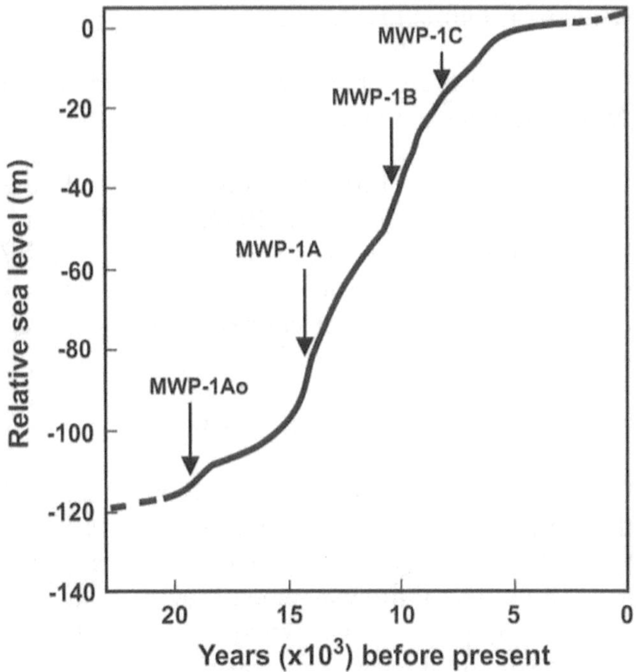

Illustration from NASA.
See link at the end of the book under 'sources'.

Imhotep tells about the explorers who left the safe and mundane life in the Lemurian areas.

"Even the 'new' Lemurians preferred to live on islands, so the city of Tien, which was northeast of what today is Cuba, was the symbol and the 'intellectual' centre of Atlantis. Atlantis had seven self-managing regions with no ruler above them, only a council."

I ask Imhotep a question that I have come up with

while he is telling his story.

"Did we use more of our brain in Lemurian and Atlantian times than we do today?"

"You're using one hundred percent of the brain. Nature is very efficient, so nothing is left dormant. It's the humans who don't USE their given brain/ mind capacity very efficiently. It's equivalent to using only a few percent of your computer's capacity."

"How did the Atlantians perceive God?"

"The Atlantians did not have a concept of God through the first and the middle periods. They were living two lives, a physical and a non-physical. The physical life was when they were awake, and the non-physical was when they were dreaming. The dream life was as real as the life they lived when they were awake. The dreams were different back then, simply because the connection to these 'dimensions' was much clearer, as was the human consciousness. You may have heard that some of the North American natives, some hundred years ago, believed that what they were dreaming was 'real'. With their limited understanding and the changes of the dream world as well as their filters to their awakened state, they often acted upon their dreams when they woke up in an inappropriate manner. They had forgotten what true dreams or visions are. To be fair, I must say that some have the true visions today. Dreams ARE real, but our mind can, for the most part, handle only three-dimensional information from our senses. The information that comes through, the brain compares to memories and knowledge and often discards it if it does not match the mind's database. That's why dreams often make no sense. They make no sense because our senses can't interpret the information if it's not already known."

"I know that I'm jumping around a little with my questions, but there is so much I would like to know; so, can you tell me something from before Lemuria?"

"If we set the start of Lemuria to when we start to incarnate, I can tell you a little of what happened before that. Life on Earth had to start five times before it was right to evolve. When the animal kingdom was flourishing, human souls first joined the animal experience as passengers, starting with the dolphins. Later the souls incarnated in animal bodies."

I sense our dialogue is finish for now, but at the same time I sense I will be given more information at a later time.

Saint Germain

I am in my flat. Again, I wake up when my alarm clock shows 7:11 and am now in the shower.

Saint Germain and the Purple Flame; it rhymes! Why do those words come into my mind?

"Well that's how I chose to present myself to you this glorious day!"

I'm moved to tears, as I feel the smile of this lovely being meeting me heart-to-heart.

"One of my friends has an interest in the Purple Flame, but it has never meant anything to me."

"That's quite all right, I'm not here to talk about the Purple Flame; it's just an aspect of what I AM, or, better said, a way through which I work."

"Why do you choose to talk to me while I'm in the shower?"

"The water clears you in many ways, and the act of clearing and cleaning gives both your mind and your body great joy. When you're joyful, you open up and invite joyful energies and consciousness to join you. Join in joy!"

"I do not feel that you are invasive."

"As you know, consciousness has no gender, and I meet you as such and not as a male or a female. I sense you as the consciousness you are; I do not see your body. And I can tell that you are far more beautiful in your light than in the human body you use as a vessel in this lifetime."

"What ARE you here to talk about?"

"You have been thinking about your father, Carl, and what he is doing for Ju-long and his family to pave the way for him and you. These thoughts bring up some threads from other lives where I was involved as well, so it invited me in. Carl Cane has never been fond of his nickname, 'CC', which could easily be pronounced "sissy", but if we look into this, it will turn out to be quite a different 'cup of tea', as you will see. The letter 'c' is the third letter of the alphabet. If you see CC as the number 33, it's the master number for, for example, Christ, or the crystal energy, or the Cristo awareness, and that is what characterises your father: a clear consciousness and genuine compassion. Furthermore, in numerology the number 3 is the catalyst, and that is exactly what your father is. Just look at what he's doing in his life: his business and investments make a lot of things possible in the world, and in a good way."

"I don't follow Dad's work in great detail, but I guess that he invests mostly in humanitarian areas."

"By the way, the name 'Carl' means 'free man'. Speaking of free men, I can tell you that both your father and you have been Freemasons in another life. The cane is a staff, not one to cling to, but a guiding tool for lighting up the path. You remember Gandalf's staff from the movies about The Ring? The guiding light at the top of the staff is for both the one holding the staff and the ones who follow the staff and the light. In a way, that is why you're the light of your parents' life. It was a message to you, a keyword, to wake something in you that you had agreed to before you were born. You're a staff of illumination, a light tower. Your awakened awareness will shine the light for humanity. The light is new ideas and a new compassion for all. Your light will shine on all the ideas and concepts that are already in the mass consciousness."

"It is kind of what Josela and Loong have told me, but it's still quite vivid to me."

"See, THIS is why we're talking. You must KNOW that this is how it works and that this IS your real work, if you want to see it as work.

"We have been working with mass consciousness many times before and in different incarnations. Consciousness took a great leap in the Renaissance in Europe and just after the end of World War Two. Though there was much cruelty during the war, there was an immense flourishing of empathy as well. This outburst of empathy showed that there is still hope for humanity to evolve."

"So, that was really what World War Two was about?"

"That, and so much more - it may be a subject for another meeting. I'll leave you now, but we'll be in touch."

"When can I expect you to visit me again?"

"Don't see it as though we're visiting you or not. We're only a 'thought' or a breath away but, in reality, YOU'RE NEVER ALONE!"

"And that's because consciousness is not a place or energy, as all of you have told me."

"Indeed!"

What a special and delightful meeting. I have got so many new true friends lately; friends that just show up and I immediately feel that I have known them forever, and probably have, but am just not aware of it.

I have finished my shower and am now checking emails, sitting on my cosy sofa with my laptop.

There is great news from Ju-long and his family. His grandparents have been promised a small flat at a retirement home, paid partly from social security and partly from a fund.

A text message sends out a 'ping' from my phone. It is my sister, Anna.

"Are you ready for a visit this afternoon? Johanne/ Jo-Ann is coming too. She's Danish. We could bring some takeaway!"

I have not seen my sister for quite some time, and I can get back home early today, so she gets a positive answer.

"You're both welcome. What kind of drink should I prepare?"

"Well, anything goes with Chinese!!! See you. Hugs, Anna."

So, Chinese it will be. Fine with me - we grew up with Chinese food as well as a quite international cuisine, partly because of au pairs from different parts of Europe and partly because Dad brought some exciting recipes back from his business trips all over the world. He enjoyed cooking with us, when he had the time. Then the whole family occupied the kitchen with Dad as 'le chef'. It's some of my best memories from my childhood.

Anna and her friend show up at five pm carrying two large, plastic bags revealing a mix of wonderful smells. Anna gives me a warm hug with her one free arm. Her friend is right behind and gives me a pleasant smile and a hug as well. She is blonde, not very tall and a little round, but without being plump. She is wearing a below-the-knee green cotton coat, a green scarf and a pair of black boots with some heel.

"I'm Johanne, but here in the UK I'm Jo-Ann; it's easier to pronounce."

"Put the bags on the coffee table in the living room."

I feel it is cosier and less formal to sit at the low table, and I have already set three places, with different glasses in the middle of the table depending on what we might choose to drink.

When Jo-Ann hangs her coat up, I see she wears beige pants and a blue shirt with buttons.

"Jo-Ann, try some of the slippers below the hangers, a pair may fit you."

Anna has medium-brown hair and a rounder body than the rest of us in the family - probably a combination of genetics from late relatives and a huge appetite. That may explain the huge bags as well. She wears blue jeans, a light-beige, knitted sweater and blue sneakers with white soles. Anna is always interested in my different works. "What are you working on at the moment?"

"I'm still researching for my book about Little People, nature spirits. I was just reading about superstitions regarding the powers of nature in China. It's interesting to see how alike the folklore of Europe, especially Ireland, and China are."

Jo-Ann asks me the next question. "Isn't it hard to read Chinese, with all those different signs?"

"Oh, I don't read it in Chinese. It is an old book written in English in Hong Kong in 1876. It's here on my tablet if you want to see it."

I turn on the tablet and hand it to Jo-Ann. After a short while she looks up, sounding very excited.

"I'm just reading about a flag falling from the sky with a particular sign on it. It reminds me of the tale of how Denmark got its flag. It happened in a battle in Estonia at the beginning of the 13th century, where a red or brown cloth with a white cross fell from the sky. The Chinese story does not talk about the colours, but the sign is a square with a cross in the middle. It says that it's the character, Tien."

"Let's look it up!" says Anna, who is always very dynamic.

After some searching, I come up with a suggestion.

"It must be the glyph, Tián, which means field. It looks like a field with irrigation canals."

On the right page in the book we see the glyph 田.

Jo-Ann's eyes widen.

"What?! Denmark means 'the fields of the Danes' or the Land of the Danes. The Danish word 'mark' means field."

I happen to look at the left page where another glyph shows a word pronounced a little differently.

"Tiān (天) is one of the oldest Chinese terms for heaven. I remember that the scientific centre of Atlantis was called Tien."

Anna did not share our excitement.

"It looks like a mere coincidence to me, with crosses, fields and flags falling from the sky."

We have a wonderful evening, and it is lovely to

spend some time with Anna, which happens too
seldom.

Sensing Your Reality

A text message comes in. It's from Ju-long.

"Finally, all formalities are in place, and my grandparents can move to the retirement home. Fantastic!"

"That's great! Do you need me to be there?"

"Yes! Not to help, but I miss you terribly!"

"I miss you too. I'll check my schedule and see when I can be in Hong Kong."

"That sounds fantastic, dear Luzi! We'll talk later."

Another text message comes in. It's from Dad.

"I've just received a message from Hong Kong: Ju-long's grandparents can move to the retirement home, and the final, practical arrangements can take place!"

"Yes, I've just heard it from Ju-long. I'll arrange a short trip to Hong Kong as soon as possible. Thanks, Dad. Say hello to Mum. Hugs, Luzi."

That is great news. Everything seems to be working out now. Hopefully, Ju-long will soon be able to move to London. I am really looking forward to being with him.

A last-minute ticket to Hong Kong makes it possible for me to arrive early on the same day as Ju-long's grandparents are scheduled to move to the retirement home.

I am now on the bus from the airport heading to Hong Kong Island. The weather is quite warm and, with the sun shining directly on the bus, the air conditioning has its problems keeping the temperature at a tolerable level. Using the bus gives me another connection to the area, better than I would get if I used a taxi. I hope that Ju-long's grandparents can settle into their new surroundings. Members of staff are there to attend to them if and when they need it, and there are small buses to take the elders out shopping and on short trips for leisure.

Loong fades into my awareness and blesses me with a warm feeling in my heart. We say hello to each other; not with words, but just feelings.

"Now you're on your way to Hong Kong Island yet again. There is a different feeling, or energy you might say, to this visit than the previous ones."

"Yes, I feel a little uneasy. Is there anything I should worry about?"

"Oh, no, you should NEVER worry, and everything is going to be fine, you'll see."

"But how come I have this feeling that something is not right?"

"You felt into the uncertainty that Ju-long, his mother and grandparents all felt, simply because

146

all of their lives are about to change, and change, as you know, can be frightening."

I want to see Loong, so I close my eyes and place my awareness in Elvendale and open my awareness eyes, if one can say that, feeling the warm sun while I am sitting on the small mound with Loong by my side. I move closer to him and place my back up against his furry side, using him as a comfortable backrest. He purrs and continues.

"New opportunities arise when one chooses to change things in one's life. Old possibilities will pull away, simply because they do not fit into the new 'energies'. It creates a space, or a vacuum, so to speak, available for new and more suitable things to come to you. In the case of the grandparents, they also have the possibility of leaving their lives entirely and returning to their natural, non-physical state of pure consciousness, that which you humans call death. Death is just a shift in consciousness and can happen quite gracefully and peacefully. The fear comes from the human part."

Sitting here in the sunshine and sensing everything around me in this magical world of Elvendale makes me want to stay forever. Loong senses my experience.

"You ARE staying here forever; a part of you is ALWAYS here and you, the consciousness, can 'be' everywhere at the same 'time'. Sorry for all the quotation marks, but there is no SPACE to STAY or BE in, and no TIME."

"What about Ju-long's mother? What is in store for

her in her new life?"

"Feel into this yourself and tell me what you sense."

Feelings come up, but it is difficult to bring them into a concept of the mind, meaning into words. It is difficult to be in two worlds at the same time - the natural world or awareness, and the 'artificial' world of the human mind. Loong helps me by presenting a suggestion.

"Imagine you are a fortune-teller relaying your sensing to your customer, in this case, Ju-long's mother."

I shift into the fortune-teller role and take an imaginary, deep breath.

"Well, with your parents being taken care of by others, you'll experience great freedom, which will allow much more energy into your life. With this surplus, you'll choose things that you previously didn't feel you could handle. These new experiences will give you even more energy, and it will start spiralling into your life. As long as you can stay balanced and not burn more energy than you allow into your life, you'll feel joyful and happy."

"Good. What if she asks you about romance in her life?"

"Hmm, I usually don't want to buy into others' love lives, but let me sense into it.

"When you feel joyful, you'll attract joyful people, people who are happy or content with themselves and their lives. They'll have the surplus to engage in a relationship for the 'right' reasons, meaning to share and not to feed on your energies."

"Excellent, Luzi."

I am pulled back into my human existence by the commotion when some people have to leave the bus a few stops from where I am going to get off. I part from Loong and prepare myself to get off the bus.

Ju-long is at the bus stop waiting for me; a warm hug and a quick kiss. He looks gorgeous! He takes my small bag, and it feels natural to let him do that without feeling any guilt or wanting to protest, because I can carry my own stuff. Loong comments on that.

"You open up to receive him into your life, and he opens up to share his life with you. He shows that now you're US, not differentiating your stuff from his."

I smile and take Ju-long's hand. I feel very happy and light in my heart. We walk to my hotel, and I check in. It takes only a few minutes; then we are back out in the sunshine, two lovebirds hovering over the sidewalk on our way to a little visit to my grandparents.

In the later years, I visited my grandparents twice a year and always felt that they had grown older each time. Lately, this year, my visits have been more frequent so now, as I hug them, I can see no difference from the last time. It is reassuring, but it is just a matter of time before my grandparents will be in the same situation as Ju-long's, and will need at least some kind of help. I am sure that Dad has made some arrangements; I must ask him next time we are in contact.

The visit is short. Ju-long and I must be off to his and his family's flat. The retirement home has provided a small truck and a driver to move their things to their new home. It is a nice service, I would say. Grandpa has fallen asleep in his chair, Grandma tells us, so only she greets us. The commotion wakes up Grandpa, and he joins us at the small, round table for tea and pancakes. It reminds me of my younger years, visiting them after school. The same atmosphere; a warm room with the sunshine coming in through the windows, the smell of an aromatic tea, hot oil, and a light scent of detergent, as Grandma always keeps the flat spotless.

Soon we are out on the street again, and Ju-long comments on the visit.

"It's always nice to visit your grandparents. There is always such harmony and light, even on a rainy day. It's very special."

"It's because you sense more than just the flat, the things and the people in it. You use more than your five senses. Your awareness picks up the energies and the feelings that have accumulated over the many years - the love, compassion, determination, and human strength. Here you feel love, not only from person to person, but also a love of life itself. It is what is lacking in your own home."

"You're right! But how do you know these things?"

"See, it's different from how you perceive life. I SENSE it to be so, which is different from knowing it in my mind. It's outside of the mind's grasp."

We arrive at the flat at the same time as the small, yellow truck with the retirement home's logo stops outside. The clock has just passed 2 pm. Ju-long talks with the driver, an elderly gentleman in a light-yellow uniform with logo, and he follows us upstairs to where Ju-long's grandparents are waiting with their belongings. His mother gives me a hug. It feels as if she is quite uneasy about the situation. We have loaded everything, and now I am a passenger in the truck, and Ju-long follows in a taxi with his grandparents. His mother stays in the flat to rearrange and do some cleaning. She will visit her parents later. The rooms seem a little larger now that some of the things have gone, and I feel it is easier to breathe here. A good cleaning and some fresh air will work miracles in the small flat.

After the two old folks are settled in and we leave them in the caring hands of the people in the retirement home, Ju-long and I pick up some takeaway food and return to his mother. She looks tired so, after dinner and tea, I suggest that Ju-long and I visit the beach.

On the way to the beach we talk about practical things in relation to him moving to London. My flat is large enough for the two of us, but we both feel that it will be all 'me', my stuff, and my arrangements that set the stage, and that he will have to fit in. He will also need a visa, a work permit and a scholarship. He will start on the work permit first thing in the morning.

Now we reach the top of the stairs down to the beach, and Ju-long asks me to go first. On the way down I can feel his eyes on my ass, and it turns me on. Down at the beach we have a few moments alone, kissing and hugging before we are interrupted by other people. Ju-long takes my hand and, while we walk, he picks up our conversation from the afternoon.

"I've been thinking about the sensing you mentioned when we talked about the difference in the atmosphere in your grandparent's flat and ours. Could you please elaborate? I feel there's a whole world I'm missing here."

I have to pull myself out of the wonderful haze I am flowing in, to answer him.

"To some degree you ARE using your 'higher' senses; you're just not aware of it, and that's the whole point, namely, awareness. You have your human senses and your human feelings; they are all related to the brain."

"Are my feelings related to my brain? I thought that feeling was related to the heart, or something like that."

I wonder how far I can go in explaining this to Ju-long, a man who is so focused on his body and mind being all that he is.

"The senses are directly linked to the brain through the neural system; sight, smell, hearing, taste and touch. The feelings, or should we call them emotions, are linked to special hormones, peptides, that are produced mainly in the brain. Each emotion has its own peptide. An emotion starts in your brain, which produces a peptide, which is then let out into the bloodstream and sent through your entire body, influencing every cell that has receptors for it. I might add that you have neurones, brain cells, all over your body, including in your heart."

"Then what about the sensing outside the brain?"

Now it begins to get tough. How do I talk about something the mind really cannot understand? I feel a deep connection and a sense of Loong, but also many others. I am not alone in this, and my friends provide me with back-ups.

"I'll give you a short version for now, because I know that we'll be talking much more in depth on this subject."

"Short is good."

"The answer is awareness. You may see it as a layer above your mind, but still energetically connected to it. You could say that it's here your intuition dwells. Here you feel or sense the world around you, while your brain receives information from your bodily senses, as well as producing emotions. As you can see, I distinguish between emotions and feelings. Emotions are a brain thing, and feelings are a sensing in your awareness."

"I hope there is not more to the short version. I've lost the grasp of this already!"

"That's all, folks, and I really need to get some rest."

"Of course; I'll walk you to the hotel, and we have three more days before you return to London."

We have a long kiss goodnight before I slip through the door into the hotel vestibule. I say goodnight to the sleepy porter and go to my room. Strangely enough, I feel completely awake and full of energy lying on the bed. I send my thanks to all who have assisted me during the day, especially during my talks with Ju-long. They must be simple and yet containing the energy or consciousness that provides the full information that will sit with him until he is ready to work on the issues in depth.

Immediately I feel a rush of love, you might say, and the message, "You're welcome!"

With tears in my eyes and love in my heart, I fall asleep, with the sense that it has been a glorious day.

Meeting the Earth and the Sun

The next morning Loong talks to me before I open my eyes, still in that state between being asleep and awake.

"I want to comment on yesterday. In the evening, you first felt tired; that was because of the many new impressions that had passed through your senses, as well as emotions and thoughts. Later on at the hotel, when you had left all this noise, you felt energised because you had channelled much information to Ju-long. You can channel only while you are open, and when you're open, the energy flows through you, as opposed to the energy that is stocked and preventing you from getting new energy to your system."

"I felt very concentrated and alert. I was thinking a lot."

"You must learn to be focused and relaxed instead of being concentrated and alert - the latter will drain your energy and overload your brain."

"I'll try to think of it, but right now my feelings for Ju-long are very much getting in the way of any sane thoughts."

"I do not say that you shouldn't enjoy your moments of insanity, I merely want you to be aware of what's happening in your system. That way, you'll be the observer in your own life, and your human part can be as lovesick as she wants."

"And she wants!"

I leave the hotel at seven am to have breakfast with Ju-long and his mother. Mrs Yu is more relaxed today.

"I'm grateful for all your help, so please give our thanks to your great father, who made this miracle come true."

The synchronicity is at work and, as if Mrs Yu has just delivered a cue, I get a text message from Dad.

"It's a text from my dad. Maybe there is something of interest for you."

Mrs Yu is eager to please me.

"Please do attend to the message, and remember to thank your dear father."

I bring up the message, hoping that there is only good news.

"Are you still in Hong Kong? I have some business there, and I also want to visit Ju-long and his family to see how they are doing in the new arrangements."

"I'm here and will leave in four days. When will you be here?"

"I'll be there the day after tomorrow, hopefully around noon. Can you tell the family that I'm showing up?"

"Indeed I will. Looking forward to seeing you. Is Mum with you?"

"No, it'll only be me this time. It's a short trip, so it would make no sense for Mum to join me."

"OK, we'll see you then."

"What flight are you on back to London? I'll try to arrange it so we can be on the same plane. I don't see you much."

Dad gets my flight number. I look forward to seeing him. As he said, we don't see much of each other.

The phone slides back into my purse, and I turn to Ju-long and his mother.

"Dad will visit Hong Kong the day after tomorrow. It's a short business trip, but he'll take the time to visit you and see how it goes at the retirement home as well. He'll try to arrange to leave on the same flight as me."

Mrs Yu brings out a big smile, but it suddenly disappears, and she looks around the apartment. Is it suitable for the visit?

"Don't worry, Mrs Yu; it looks fine. Some flowers on the table, an aromatic tea and some cookies, and he'll feel that you greet him like royalty."

We finish breakfast and Mrs Yu leaves for her job at the mall. It takes some persuasion to let Ju-long and I clean up, but finally we are alone. Ju-long has to be at the library at ten, but we have some time to talk about our common future.

Well, that was my intention, but we are spending most of the time kissing and hugging, and I am ready to explode with lust, when Ju-long's alarm goes off to tell us that it is time to go to the library. I follow him to the front door of the library. It is a warm day, and I float on imaginary clouds with his hand in mine, his scent in my nose and a sore tongue from rubbing against my front teeth during our kissing. We do not speak. I leave him in front of the library and continue my walk to visit my grandparents. My body is vibrating from all the hormones still pumping through it.

At my grandparents, I am far away in my thoughts and feelings. They understand my situation, and we are just sitting in the small living room enjoying the warmth from the sun shining through the windows. I gaze at the shadows of the curtains that slowly move across the top of the table as the sun follows its path across the sky.

Later, we take a short walk to the stairs down to the beach. Grandpa has a good day, but he does not want to take on the steep stairs. I, having no plans, decide to take a walk along the shoreline.

"I think I'll take a walk on the beach, and may be back at teatime. Otherwise, I'll pick up Ju-long after he has finished his work at 5 pm."

Grandpa nods and Grandma smiles and takes my hand.

"A lot has happened in your life lately. A walk

along the beach will do you good and clear your thoughts and feelings. We see you when we see you."

I kiss them both and descend to the stony beach via the stairs with trees on each side as well as steel bannisters painted light blue. The small waterfall to my right makes quite some noise. As my feet touch the beach, I feel Loong's presence.

"Now that you are walking on the beach, feel into the awareness of this place. I don't mean using your body's senses, but your sensory awareness. Like the way you sense when your focus is in Elvendale. It may take a little while to get into this mode, since you're used to using the senses of your body."

The first that comes to me is a sense of the rocks around me, not only the stones on the seashore but the rock foundation of the whole island and into the sea. It feels alive; it has awareness! Patience, slowness; like the life of a mountain, from its rising from the ground and growing to its heights and, at the same time, its constant erosion. The rock is not truly hard, but fragile, always in decay. I feel a cycle like slow-moving lava, always shifting, always changing.

"It's amazing!"

"Now communicate with the rocks, but use your awareness, not your mind."

I open my sensory awareness, and I am almost knocked over by a grand wash of love. I can only describe it as The Love of the Mother. I connect with the planet itself. Tears start to run down my face, and I sit down on a large, smooth stone, which reminds me that rocks certainly are mouldable. It is now a very gentle and nurturing 'energy' I sense. Loong whispers gently to me.

"All that you just called energy are real feelings picked up by your sensory awareness. You can call it your soul's sensory feelings, in contrast to your body's senses. The soul's senses are feelings, not physical senses or emotions."

"So when I see a mountain, or even this planet, it's not what it seems. It's just how it presents itself in the physical world."

"A mountain in the human world does not 'look' like a physical mountain in mine. When you 'looked' with your consciousness, you 'saw' patience and slowness. That's the rudimental 'picture' of the mountain in the Sidhe world or, better said, the melody or the song of a mountain."

I am just sitting here, sensing into the world, letting myself calm down and enjoying being in existence. After a while some seagulls catch my attention, and I check my watch. It is time to go back to Grandma and assist her with the shopping. I send a conscious nod to the place, as a thank-you for the connection, and leave the beach. I meet Grandma outside the entrance to the block. She leans towards her trolley, talking to the caretaker, Mr Wu. I greet them both, and then Grandma and I go shopping, me manoeuvring her trolley. After shopping, being back in my grandparents' apartment, I make a lunch pack for

Ju-long and me, because we had planned to meet on his lunch break at the library. It will be a nice surprise for him.

"Grandma, I surely hope that Ju-long's grandparents will settle in at the retirement home."

"Yes indeed; it has given both his mother and himself a lot more freedom to choose what they want in their lives. I'm sure they will. The retirement home sounds like a nice place, with an excellent staff."

I make some sandwiches and get two bottles of Grandma's home-made ginger ale, fruits and hard-boiled eggs. I have packed everything in a nice basket so the contents will not crush. I even get a table cloth so that it can be a real picnic!

"Don't forget cutlery and napkins, Luzi!"

"Oh yes, of course! Well, not the cutlery; it won't be necessary."

"And glasses!"

"We'll drink from the bottles."

I kiss Grandpa, who is sitting in his armchair, and Grandma, before I rush out of the door. I almost knock over Mr Wu, who just happens to pass the door at the same moment as I slam it open.

"Sorry, Mr Wu, have a nice day!"

"And a beautiful day to you, Miss Cane."

I reach the library well in time and decide to wait outside. There is a small ledge below the notice board where I can sit. Even though the street is narrow, the sunshine can find its way to me. I decide to connect to the sun and, even before I am quite sure if I will do it, I feel a great wash of love, just as I did when connecting to the Earth.

"The Earth is the life-giver from below, and I am the Life-Giver from above. You're all loved by both your Earth-mother and your Sun-father, though we're not your parents. We are entities, consciousness with a purpose, as you are."

I am overwhelmed and do not know what to say.

"Blessings, Sun."

"Blessings, dear. Don't see me as a big ball of fire; that's just a function I have. As I said, I'm consciousness. I know who you are, and I've been following you. Not your day-to-day life, but your song; you may call it the song of your soul, your real name, your colours."

"But how can you be following me?"

"Oh, you as a person think you're too small to be noticed and, in that sense, you're right. I see your light as the light tower you are. I recognise your name in colours from long before you became an embodied entity."

I am utterly speechless, and my mind stops. All there is is ME and the connection to this loving consciousness. At this moment I can sense what I am, and it is not my body, or my mind and feelings. What a wonderful experience in pure beingness, if such a word exists.

Ju-long almost falls over my feet when he comes out from the library.

"You're crying! What's wrong?"

"They are tears, but I'm definitely not sad. I'm happy! And I bring lunch, so let's find a nice spot in the park!"

Ju-long gives me a long hug and a quick kiss.

"You had me worried there for a second, Luzi."

He takes the basket in one hand and my hand in the other, and we walk to Waterfall Bay Park, which is just a strip of grass with some trees around and some concrete benches but, when turning our view to the sea, it gives the illusion of being in nature. The illusion is spoiled each time a motorised vehicle passes behind us, or a container ship passes in front of us.

We have a lovely picnic, and I love being with Ju-long. I am so much looking forward to being with him in London. Our talk is not too serious, and we simply enjoy each other's company and the food.

Quan Yen

After following Ju-long back to the library, I go back to the beach. I see different items washed up on the shore, most of them made of plastics. I wonder why no one from the authorities keeps the beach below the park clean. I sit down on the same smooth rock I used this morning. It is quite warm, heated up by the warmth of the sun. Now it seems natural to speak to the rocks; well, the beach itself.

"Sorry about the mess we humans are putting on you. I wish I could do something."

"You can, but I wouldn't suggest getting a plastic sack and starting to pick up all the stuff. We have people to do that!"

It is Josela. I first recognise her perfume, and then I see her smiling face for my inner eyes.

"Hello, Josela, nice of you to drop by!"

"As you know, I'm kind of always here, and this is a perfect opportunity for you to practise a little. I'll ask you just to acknowledge the items that don't belong here on the beach, without any judgement. Forget about past and future; it's just this moment. I use the term 'item' so as not to put any judgement on it, as I will do if I say garbage, or even shit!"

"Yes, I can feel the difference, and I don't like the word 'shit'."

"Now imagine how the beach would look without

the items. Then let the vision go and turn your focus back to me."

It is easy for me to imagine the small beach without the plastic bottles and the other stuff. Then I turn to Josela, and we are now sitting in an altered reality where she is sitting in front of me at the beach.

"It's good to see you again, Josela. So much has happened since we talked the last time."

"Yes, I know, without having spied on you."

"Now that Ju-long's grandparents have moved to the retirement home, everything seems brighter and, hopefully, Ju-long can move to London soon so that we can live together."

"Your cheeks are blushing, and your eyes are shining. It's wonderful to see!"

"Well, thanks."

I can feel my face warm up. I look at Josela's eyes. Are they more blue than green today? I haven't said it, but Josela answers as if I have spoken it out loud.

"Just because I appear in human form doesn't mean that we're not meeting as consciousness. There's no thought here, just consciousness. And yes, have you forgotten the small altar for Quan Yen not far from here?"

A beautiful woman appears beside Josela, dressed in a shiny, blue silk kimono, her black hair gath-

166

ered in at the back of her head.

"Greetings! As you can guess, I am Quan Yen."

"Hello. Of course, I remember the altar, but I've always seen it as superstitious nonsense. Sorry."

"Well, you did look differently at it in your younger days. We had some talks back then. Not in words, but in feelings. I'll withdraw from this meeting but, as you know, we can always connect, and we'll meet sooner than you know."

"We'll do that."

She vanishes from my eyes, not with a puff, but with a quick fade. Her body has hidden two men in beige uniforms who slowly approach us from the south. What are they doing?

As they come closer I can see that each of them is carrying a big bag made of sacking, and handling a gripping tool, picking up things from the ground and placing them in the bag.

"Look, the two men are cleaning up the beach!"

"The power of imagination, consciousness and synchronicity."

"Well, that was fast!"

"Consciousness works outside of time and space, but you can now experience how easy it can be to make changes in the human world."

"Wow, yes. But how do you do this in the Sidhe world?"

"Well, there is no garbage in the first place but, as I've told you and showed you, we use our imagination with our creative consciousness to change or create things."

"Oh, yes, of course."

"I'll close this meeting, but we shall meet again."

Josela gives me a hug and a kiss on each cheek. It is so wonderful being with her again. Just as with Quan Yen, it was a quick meeting, with the ending quite abrupt.

"Say hello to Loong for me."

"As if I'm not here!"

I feel Loong's presence as well as his jolly smile and the warm hug.

"Sorry, friend; I always forget the depth of the REAL world."

I stand up, starting to follow the beach on my way to the concrete stairs up to my grandparents' block. Shortly after, I can hear the small waterfall pouring down the cliff. Even without thinking about it, I greet the waterfall, and it greets me back!

"We have spent countless hours together, me carrying your tiny 'boats' down the small stream and out into the sea. We were all here with you as we are now - the water, the trees and insects, the rocks, the Sun; even the air around you and, occasionally, the rain."

It is not said in words, but conveyed in feelings, with consciousness.

Now I can see the altar painted in a light blue colour, the same colour as the bannister on the stairs. The altar, built of rocks and concrete, is close to an old tree that completely covers it from above with its branches and leaves.

The blue lady, Quan Yen, Goddess of Mercy, feels very present and I give her an imaginary nod, as I pass the altar.

Then I have to stop, because she gives me a gentle hug and conveys a message to me.

"I speak to you as the consciousness they call Quan Yen, as well as the Gaia. We are in close contact with the Sidhe, and we'll use this opportunity where you're very open to us communicating with you."

I am overwhelmed by this lovely present and very curious about what will come.

"As you may know, Gaia is the overall consciousness that agreed to bring this planet into existence for the human experience or, more correctly, the soul experience in a slowed-down reality, now being as slow as thoughts. As the human awareness, the consciousness, awakes, it's time for humanity to take over the baton as the overseer of this creation. We've done our part and are slowly letting go of our focus on this creation, to give it free as a sovereign creation for humanity to manage. It's done with the utmost love and honour, and with all our best wishes for what may come."

Gaia is leaving! I get an uneasy feeling; can we manage this very complex system on our own?

"We wouldn't leave the baton to you if we weren't sure you could manage it. The whole support system of entities will stay with you, continuing their development as part of THEIR journey. Some of them will leave with us and things will change and rearrange; but they have to, since it's another consciousness that'll be in charge."

"But where will you go?"

"As you've heard, consciousness doesn't GO anywhere but, in human terms, I'm just getting a new job. Not in the meaning of work, but a new hobby or interest, you might say."

"Do you REALLY mean that the human race is ready and capable of doing this?!"

"Remember that it's not the human psyche or mind that is in charge, but the consciousness or, as you might say, the soul, that'll be the boss."

I feel yet another warm hug and then their presence pulls back, leaving me at the bottom of the stairs with the light blue bannister leading to Waterfall Bay Road above. Has this really happened? Am I the right person to carry this burden of knowing that we have to take a hundred percent responsibility for the planet? I feel the waterfall close behind me, sending me a kind smile.

"Oh yes. Remember that only an insignificant part of this experience is a human being. The human is just the anchor point for you, the soul, in this 3D reality."

"I'm still not confident with the thought. I hope we'll clean you up, though, because frankly, you don't smell very nice."

"You hit it right on. It is exactly what may change! You can smell and see that things could be better and, by you being aware of the conditions, things will change. Isn't that great?!"

"That's what you all say, but it just seems so over-whelming. I mean, SO MUCH has to change; you're just a tiny waterfall, a drop in the ocean, literally."

"I'm NOT the waterfall, but consciousness; but you're right; a lot could change for the better - that's why we start with you, and humans like you. You're still few, but enough to start the snowball rolling down the hill, getting larger and larger and therefore gaining momentum. This momentum will tip the balance and set things in motion. You can be sure of that. Remember that another snow-ball started to roll two thousand six hundred years ago, when the Christ consciousness came in; not to compare the two in any way."

"I think it clears things a bit. I thank you and bid you farewell for this time."

"And farewell to you, dear Lucia!"

As I climb the stairs, I realise that the words I have been using in these last conversations have not been those I usually use. It is like they are coming from somewhere else.

Loong pops in with a comment, and I can feel his fluffy fur against my face.

"Your normal voice is just the human one but, as you now know, you've many voices from many lives."

"I don't seem to remember any of them."

"You don't have to remember them. That's just a mental thing. Your lives are shining out into this, very special life; the life of 'coming together'. By the way, did you notice that the waterfall called you by your birth name, Lucia? It did that to tell you that you're one of those who'll light up the things that people could attend to."

I go back to my grandparents, return the basket, clean up and have a cup of tea with Grandma. Grandpa is sleeping in his chair. When he wakes up I will follow him downstairs, where he will pick up his newspaper and return to the flat to enjoy it with a cup of tea.

What Is Love?

I go to the hotel to shower and change clothes. I feel both very alive and, at the same time, very tired. I lie down on the bed, feeling that I am drifting into sleep even before my head touches the pillow.

A smell of grass, pine trees and moist soil makes me open my eyes. I'm in Elvendale, just outside the tree-line of a forest, on one of the lush meadows. Loong is right beside me and, when he sees me, he rolls over and shows me his fluffy belly, encouraging me to rub it - playful and mature at the same time. I remember our conversation about dragons and knights, and pose him a question while I am rubbing his belly.

"We've been talking about the virtues of the knights, but we didn't touch on the concept of love. What is love?"

"You could say that love is a headline for many different feelings, primarily directed to someone or something 'outside' the self. Remember that feeling is a chemical release into the bloodstream from the brain, causing a sensory experience in the body, and is derived from the thoughts, or thought forms usually retrieved from your memory, triggered by an outside event; a RE-action."

"Love can be a strong feeling of connection with another being, but the way you say it makes it sound very cold and clinical, if I can use that phrase!"

"Well, it is; but humans ARE emotional beings, so

it feels very real, and to the human it IS real. A human IS thoughts and feelings. It's actually a very simple construction: a physical body and a system that reacts to incoming stimuli. It may have some level of self-awareness, but usually without any understanding of the whole picture. Some humans have a faint feeling or just a wish that there were something more to life."

Loong is right. And especially those who believe in a God see themselves as a person with a soul, meaning that they are primarily a person; and then there is something called a soul somewhere, as well as a supreme being in control. That is why bodies were, and are, embalmed, and people have a picture of being given a (new) body when resurrected. They ARE their body, without any REAL concept of what the soul is. How can humanity wake up from this grand illusion?

I wake up to this human reality at a quarter to 5 pm, just in time to get to the library to pick up Ju-long.

We have chosen to make dinner at Ju-long's place, so we go out shopping before going to the apartment. After dinner, we will go to see a movie in Cyberport Broadway Theatres.

When dining, I address Ju-long's mother.

"Mrs Yu, when you're visiting your parents this evening, could you please tell them that Ju-long and I will join you tomorrow, visiting them as well? Then, when my father arrives the day after tomorrow, only you and he will visit, so that it won't be a crowd."

"That may be a good idea. I'll tell my parents, dear Luzi."

When Mrs Yu leaves to visit her parents, Ju-long and I take some short cuts to the Telegraph Bay area, reaching the Broadway Theatres, which are in a huge, circular building containing four houses, with more than eight hundred seats. A ticket costs about eight British Pounds.

I do not remember what movie was; I am not there to enjoy the movie, but to feel Ju-long close to me, holding my hand in the dark. After the movie, we slowly walk through Cyberport Waterfront Park. Ju-long walks me back to my hotel. Tomorrow we will visit his grandparents, and I hope they have settled in.

With great joy in my tummy and love in my heart, I tuck myself in, knowing that everything will work out fine.

A scent is tickling my nose; COFFEE. I open my eyes and see Josela looking down at me, sitting beside me on the grass in Elvendale. She has Loong on her lap, not as a dragon, but as a Birman cat like the first time I saw him at Josephine's grandma in Shanghai. I get up into a sitting position.

"I sense your happiness," Loong says, and walks over to me.

"Yes, I had a wonderful evening with Ju-long. Now I feel that things are starting to work out for us."

Even though I have been here in Elvendale several times, I am astounded by how more rich and alive everything feels here, and feel sad that the human senses are so limited.

Loong rubs his head against my hand, tickling my face with his raised tail while purring.

"You must use your other senses to get a fuller experience to notice that EVERYTHING is alive in your three-dimensional world as well."

Josela continues. "You've felt the mountains, the Earth and the Sun, and have communicated with their consciousness. Even the small waterfall has touched you. Now there should be no doubt for you, that everything has consciousness but not necessarily a human soul. The degree of awareness varies from entity to entity, from the elementary entity which takes care of a single flower, to the highly evolved consciousness of a star, the Sun."

"How can we, the humans, master such a high consciousness so that we can take over from Gaia?"

Loong says, "There is, and will be, places of low consciousness on the planet. Some people will feel themselves drawn to these places, so the Earth itself won't suffer, it'll only be the local humans there, who'll live their lives in low awareness, but they'll still have the possibility of connecting to a higher consciousness when they're ready. Those humans who're born in such areas have a matching consciousness, or a few are born in the area simply to bring a higher awareness to the general population. They usually have a hard life, simply because they feel that they don't belong there. Hopefully, they'll find out why they are there."

I see a man coming towards us, crossing the plains from the forest. When he comes closer, I see that he is dressed elegantly in 1700s garments, probably French fashion from that period. Quite handsome, I would say.

"Blessings; I am Comte Saint Germain of Saint Germain."

We greet him as he takes a seat on a tree stump that seems to appear at the moment he sits down. I notice that he wears a very nice pair of boots.

"Your subject is taking a turn that is of utmost interest to me, and I am monitoring it closely. I'll therefore, with your permission, participate in this discussion."

"Yes, please; I need some clarification on this subject. But first, tell me why you presented yourself as Comte Saint Germain of Saint Germain?"

"I'm greeting you as the aspect Comte Saint Germain of the consciousness, Saint Germain, and I'm afraid my comments will raise more questions; but, at the same time, you must have more pieces of the puzzle to carry on, so listen carefully."

He makes a dramatic pause before he continues.

"Humanity is moving away from nature, from Gaia. Humanity is moving away from being animals to being a being where consciousness AND body, mind and emotions combine into what we could call a 'body of consciousness'. These beings will be aware of their true creative abilities from the consciousness, and still be living in a physical, three-dimensional world, just like the Sidhe are now in their non-physical world."

"There are a lot of changes in the world; not all for the better, as far as I can see. What has that to do with this shift you're talking about?"

"A part of this shift, where Gaia leaves, you can see in the fact that a lot of species are leaving the planet; they become extinct, leaving a space so new species can come in. You see it in the decline of some of the large carnivores."

"And what will then keep the herbivores in check, if the large carnivores disappear?"

"The bees are leaving as well, and new ways for plants to pollinate will appear. The same will happen regarding the herbivores."

"Is it similar to when the Bible is talking about the lion and the lamb living side by side?"

"Well, you might say that, but you shouldn't bring religion into this. Religion is a human-made illusion. YOU are the creator. Let us come back on track. As Gaia and Quan Yen told you yesterday, a whole new system will come into this creation, so life will have to change considerably, when we manage the planet differently."

"It may sound exciting but, to me, it sounds very

scary. What if it doesn't work?"

Saint Germain stands up, starting to pace slowly back and forth in front of us.

"It's the same consciousness creating the new world that created the old one. It's the same designer and the same craftsmen who are at work. Everything will find its natural harmony, or what you might call balance."

"Why can't we just stick to what we have?"

"Are you really satisfied with how things are? Creation HAS TO move on; stagnation is equivalent to degradation, which will lead to the end of this creation."

"If we live forever, what will happen if this creation ends?"

"When this creation ends it will turn into itself, implode and, from the ashes, a new creation will rise. It will be much more than just this solar system, this galaxy and this universe; it'll be every THING that ceases to exist! We can't let this 'small' piece determine the fate of the rest of creation. That's to say that what happens to Earth is influencing the rest of creation. Creation will continue, wave after wave, until there is no more water in its sea, so to speak; water being opportunities."

My intellect cannot grasp this vastness, so I sit with feelings that I haven't experienced before, quite numb and empty in my head. It is kind of nice; there is just a feeling of knowingness. Now I slip into nothingness.

I wake up quite early; early enough to have break-fast with my grandparents. They are excited to meet Dad as well. He and I will return to England on the same plane. He has even arranged a seat be-side mine! I long to be with him tomorrow, and we, Ju-long and I, may need a little help with getting Ju-long a place to live.

At this point I cannot tell what I was doing in the period between breakfast with my grandparents and picking up Ju-long at the library at 5 pm. I just remember that he came running towards me, wav-ing a piece of paper in his right hand, shortly be-fore I reached the library.

"I've got the work permit! I've got the work per-mit!"

He reaches me, grabs me and lifts me up, kissing me. Then he has to put me down again to catch his breath. I read the paper, and he is right.

"But I would expect it to take months?!"

Loong smiles at me. "Synchronicity, my dear; syn-chronicity."

I send texts to Mum and Dad to give them the news. We go to the mall to tell Mrs Yu the good news. She is busy at the cash register, and I can sense that she is both happy and sad at the same time; happy on her son's behalf, and sad because the time when he will leave her for England is coming closer. Ju-long invites both of us out to dinner.

At the restaurant, Mrs Yu is quiet most of the time. Ju-long and I talk excitedly about our future. Later, on our way to Ju-long's grandparents, I manage to settle my excitement a bit, and now we arrive at the entrance of the retirement home.

The entrance looks anonymous, but once we are inside there is an inviting lobby with a receptionist at a counter. She smiles at us, eager to be of service. We take the elevator and, shortly after, Ju-long knocks at door number 315. The sum of the digits is 9, meaning 'completion'. I had not thought of that when I helped to move their things into the flat. The old man opens the door, greets us with a warm smile, and seems happy to see us.

"Come in, come in. Nice to see you again, Luzi!"

"Thank you, Mr Lin; I look forward to hearing how things are working out for both of you in your new surroundings."

Mrs Lin comes out and greets us as well. I see that there is more life in her eyes than the last time I saw her. I'm very pleased about that. Ju-long breaks the news about his work permit even before the front door is closed. The old people look happy on his behalf.

"Now you need to find a good job, but don't be picky, a better job may turn up later!" Mr Lin lowers his index finger again and shows us to the low table in the living room, already covered with tableware. Mrs Lin is just able to squeeze in the dish with home-made cake in the middle of it.

It is a small flat, although larger than my grandparents'. They tell about common rooms and facilities, which compensate for the small space. I comment on the cake.

"A lovely cake, Mrs Lin."

"Yes indeed. This afternoon, some of us older women from the block met in the large kitchen below, making all sorts of cakes and cookies. We had such a joyful time."

It is nice to hear that she has found new friends. I grab the moment to state why this visit is so important to me.

"As you know, my father will visit you tomorrow, together with your daughter. It is vital that you tell him if there is anything you don't like. He'll not see it as you complaining about his arrangement for you, he just wants to be sure that you have got what was promised. It's his business gene, I suppose. He'll be very diplomatic when he points out things to the manager, so you won't be discredited for complaining."

Mr Lin smiles and looks me in the eyes.

"It's a wonderful place, and it has brought new life into our relationship. As you can hear, Grandma is doing all kinds of stuff, and I have got some lovely friends for chatting. At the weekend, we'll travel to the Repulse Bay Beach. Not that I would lay in the sun, swim or anything; I'll probably find a nice place in the shade. I'll have a look at the temple and the statues."

"It'll be a nice picnic. Some of us will do the shopping and others will prepare the food," Mrs Lin adds.

We don't stay too long. Ju-long's mother joins us part of the way, and when Ju-long kisses me goodnight in front of the hotel, everything spins in me, both thoughts and feelings. I am very happy.

Dad's Surprise

It is the day of my dad's arrival in Hong Kong. I'm at my grandparents' place, and we are all three of us waiting for him. He calls from the airport, where he has arrived on the night plane as scheduled. He has hired a car and is now on his way to Hong Kong Island. Grandma has been busy in the kitchen all morning, preparing a late lunch for just the three of us. She is not stressed in any way but moves around, humming while she does her stuff. I am allowed to do some of the mundane tasks, but the details and the finesse must be done by La Chef only. Grandpa has not taken a nap today, and is sitting in his armchair reading a newspaper. It is very much as in the earlier days, and I feel very safe and happy.

The door bell rings, and it is my dad. I rush out of the door but do not get far before Dad takes me in his arms. It is so good to see him again. We walk the narrow stairs up, arm in arm. Grandma takes off her apron, wipes her hands on it, and hangs it on a hook on the wall behind the kitchen door before she receives a warm hug.

"So good to see you, Grandma. And what a smell!"

"And to see you, Carl. You look great."

"Welcome, Carl."

"Grandpa!"

They shake hands.

Grandma and Grandpa do not need anything in their lives, so Dad's gift for them is that he has re-charged their personalised Octopus bus card for another year and got them some free entertainment passes, like Disneyland Hong Kong and different sites in the area.

We have a great lunch. Dad entertains us with some of his latest news, and we talk about the time when we all lived in Hong Kong. Dad and I stay all afternoon until after dinner. Grandpa enjoys talking with Dad. Grandma would normally not allow Dad to help her and me with the dinner, but Dad is the 'head' of the family, and his parents-in-law have become used to him doing all kinds of homey things, simply because they see that he enjoys it.

After dinner, Dad and I drive to Ju-long and his mother. It isn't far, but Dad likes the freedom. When we arrive, I press the door bell and, when we stand at the door to the flat, Dad wants to be first to say hello.

Mrs Yu is dressed in a long-sleeved, quite colourful dress, reaching below her knees, with yellow as the base colour. Added to all this are a broad, black belt and a necklace of pink pearls.

"Welcome, Mr Cane, and thank you for all your help. We are very grateful."

Dad puts on his charming smile. "Hello, Mrs Yu; I'm glad that I could be of some help. Oh, I have a small thing for you."

He hands her a small package in a golden wrap

with embossed roses.

It is a very beautiful, hand-crafted pendant made of green jade, showing some beautiful ornamentation. It has a chain in gold. In addition to this, there are two earrings and a ring in the same style.

"Oh, but they must have been quite expensive, Mr Cane!"

"Well, I suppose, since we're soon to be family, if Ju-long and Luzi can figure out the details, I would say it's appropriate. I hope the ring fits, otherwise I'll change it for you."

Mrs Yu turns to her son. "Take a look, Ju-long; it's really beautifully crafted."

While Ju-long occupies his mother, I see Dad pull out an envelope from an inside pocket of his jacket. "I have something for you too, Ju-long," and hands him the envelope.

By the look on Dad's face, I can tell that he is very pleased with himself. Ju-long opens the envelope with me looking over his shoulder. There is a logo at the top of the letter, and I recognise it as belonging to the company that runs the rental of flats where I live in London. I read it fast and shout out loud, "It's a contract for a flat in the very same block in which I live in London!"

"It only needs your signature, Ju-long," Dad says with a smile. "Now that you have a work permit, I see no reason why you shouldn't move to London."

Wow, what a surprise! Now I know that THIS was Dad's business in Hong Kong. He wanted to deliver the surprise himself.

Ju-long doesn't know what to say. "What can I say?"

"'Thank you, Mr Cane,' would be just fine." Dad smiles.

"Yes, of course. Thank you very much, Mr Cane. It means a lot to me; well, us."

Mrs Yu turns to Dad. "Mr Cane, you're a big spender today. Ju-long has been talking so much about moving to London. Would you like something? Tea, perhaps?"

"Please, no, Mrs Yu. We'll probably get tea at your parents' place. Maybe it's time to leave the young ones here?"

"Oh, sure; I'll be ready in a minute! Just need my shoes and the coat."

Dad is one big smile. It's nice to see him so relaxed and full of energy.

When they leave, I catch Dad's eyes while forming the words 'thank you'. It's of course for the flat in London.

Ju-long and I have some time alone together. Of course there is some intense kissing and hugging, but soon we sit sketching a serious plan for our future. Ju-long has very few things that he wants to take with him to London. All the rest will be easy to get when he arrives. The first thing will be to get him an initial job, and the second a scholarship. We have already made a list of libraries that may be interested in his knowledge of Chinese language and culture. I have my private wish: that the university hires him, adding him to the teaching staff after he has attended some courses. We agree that he should move to London as soon as he can leave his job at the library here.

We agree that now we must use some energy on preparing his mother, for this will indeed become a great change in her life as well as having her parents leaving the flat.

Mrs Yu and Dad return. We make some small talk. Dad mentions how nice he finds it that Mrs Yu's parents have settled in their new home, and I say to her that Ju-long can't move to England right away because of his job at the library. Dad will return the signed papers and will keep the flat paid for until Ju-long arrives. Then Dad and I leave for the hotel.

We use the small hotel close to my grandparents' home, as a convenience and not because it is fancy in any way. We have known the manager for quite some years, and we have a great relationship.

Before we drive to the hotel, we park at the harbour for a walk along the Aberdeen Promenade, starting at the west end just after the fish market. We see the junks, boats and small yachts. As usual, people are waiting at the Jumbo Floating Restaurant ferry pier. Dad tells me about the visit, and we talk about my grandparents. It may not be so far in the future before Grandpa will need more care than Grandma can provide. Then I get an idea.

"How about we all have dinner tomorrow at some restaurant? Then Grandma and Grandpa will have a good chance to hear how the retirement home is. It may make them more eager to visit the place."

"A very good idea, Luzi!"

"I'll text Ju-long to let him spread the invitation to his family. We'll talk to Grandma and Grandpa in the morning."

Young couples on dates are sitting on the benches constructed like small junks, with a canopy to give shade during the warm hours. We pass a nice play-ground, where a few children are having fun.

"Well, Dad, what was your gift for Ju-long's grand-parents?"

"That was a tough one! For some strange reason, I ended up buying a small dragon altar for their new home. I dismissed the idea a couple of times, but kept on returning to the altar."

"I think it's a very appropriate thing to give them. It shows that you wish them a harmonious home. Maybe some dragon has already moved in!"

Dad does not believe in dragons, but he surely wishes them a nice home. We drive back to the hotel and Dad kisses me goodnight. We have arranged to have breakfast at my grandparents' place. Back in my hotel room, Ju-long texts me that they are all in for the dinner invitation tomorrow, and ends his message with, "I'm so happy. We'll soon be together in London! Kisses!"

What happens over the next few days before Dad and I return to London, I'll tell briefly. The dinner with all of us participating goes quite well. The older folk seem to get along very well, and they arrange for my grandparents to visit the retirement home to see the place and, of course, the flat. Dad calls the retirement home to ensure they get the most out of it, without letting them feel that it is a promotion. Ju-long sends emails to some libraries in London, applying for job interviews. I plan to make a small tour myself, visiting some of them where I have some good contacts.

After spending so much time with Dad I really miss mum, so I visit my parents a few days after getting back to London. My sister, Anna, is in Egypt.

It is so good to visit my parents in their lovely home outside London. To some extent, the interior looks like our home in Hong Kong in my younger years, and the smells are identical.

Mum and I bake a cake for our afternoon tea. While it is in the oven I am sitting on a chair in the kitchen with my eyes closed, and the smell brings back memories from my childhood in China.

Mum is creating some traditional Chinese paintings which have become quite popular and which are sold through one of her contacts in London. They usually have a romantic motif with a short text in traditional Chinese letters. It gives me the opportunity to talk about the signs I am using in my book.

"They're not the Chinese letters you'll use in your paintings, Mum."

"No, but I think you should try to write them, and feel the energy they provide. I'll fetch some good pieces of paper and ink, and we'll draw them together."

Mum shows me how to draw the lines in the right order and, when I feel into a sign while creating it, I sense they each have a unique feel to them. They have a kind of awareness, or personality. It is not the sign itself that is alive, but what it represents.

"It is remarkable how different they feel. I can almost imagine a small imp jumping up and down, trying to get my attention."

"Luzi, it reminds me of a small book I have somewhere. Let me see if I can find it."

Shortly after, she returns with a small book titled The Hidden Messagers in Water written by a Japanese doctor named Masaru Emoto. He studies how messengers, or just single words invoked on water, will change the look of the ice crystals that form when the water is frozen. Water will even change when a word is written on a label and placed on the sample bottle. His message is that, since 75% of the adult human body is water, we are very susceptible to written and spoken words and sounds. Just think what a song can do to you. It will actually make physical changes in your body!

Dad joins us at teatime, and he and I tell Mum about his visit to Hong Kong, our time with Grandma and Grandpa, and the meeting with Ju-long and his family. In all this, and being with my parents, I can feel the connection back to my childhood.

We have a wonderful day, and I am not in a hurry to get back to London; so now I have arrived at my flat, and it is quite late. I feel really happy and am looking forward to Ju-long's arrival and our new lives in the UK.

Ju-long in London

With joy in my heart and tears in my eyes, I run towards Ju-long, who is pulling a suitcase and carrying a backpack. He sees me and starts running towards me, smiling his wonderful smile. His backpack jumps up and down. We end our slalom between people, luggage and benches in a warm embrace.

"At last, you're here!"

"Yes, at last, and with all my precious belongings!"

"They may be precious, but not valuable as far as I can recall."

"It's so good to be here finally!"

"I have one of my dad's cars. It's easier than carrying your things in the trains but probably slower. Let's move to our new lives together!"

First we talk a lot but, after a while, the conversation stops and we sit, sensing each other in a very deep way. I switch myself to 'auto-pilot' and enjoy the moment that I wish would go on forever.

We arrive at the block. I have a parking lot in the parking cellar but do not use it often. When I moved in some years ago, Mum and Dad gave me some shares in the building complex, so the rent is not that high, and it includes the parking lot. Mum and Dad knew that I wanted to pay my rent myself but, as I couldn't afford it at that time, they disguised their support with the shares. I have added more shares later.

In the elevator I handed Ju-long his access key token to his front door. The flat is quite empty, since I want him to create his home totally by himself. As I said to him: "It's YOUR flat!"

I have, of course, sneak peeked, but now we explore the rooms arm in arm. Ju-long turns me around so we are standing face to face, looking into each other's eyes.

"I'm SO happy; I need a few days to figure out how to furnish my place - I don't want to rush it."

"I know, and to save you the trouble of measuring it all up I have a drawing in my flat."

"So you've already had your thoughts about my place!" He smiles.

"Well, I see some possibilities and am ready to give my support, but it's entirely up to you. When you've seen what you need to, let's go upstairs to my place; I have a small dinner almost prepared!"

"Well, if there is dinner with a beautiful young woman, I wouldn't let her wait!"

He kisses me, and we walk hand in hand to the elevator. Soon I can welcome him into my home.

"Wow, that's a kind of place; and larger than mine! I can explore this place; I just need a GPS and some gear!"

"There have been people who have found it a bit messy, but I say it gives a lot of atmosphere to the place."

"Here IS atmosphere; I really like it."

"Save the exploration until later and open the wine at the table."

"Yes ma'am! I'm on it."

We have arranged a small computer with a video link to Ju-long's mother so, as the food is cooking in the oven, we have a delightful conversation with her before she goes to bed.

We have a wonderful evening. When I empty the wine bottle into our glasses, I mention that Ju-long has to sleep here, since he has no bed. Did I plan this?

"Unless you have a sleeping mat in your suitcase! I really don't want you to spend your first night in London in an empty flat."

"Thanks, I find it cosier here, and the company is much better."

This first night together could be a standard for any romantic bride's wedding night. We shared each other in the most intimate way, and with such a deep connection. To me, this was a reunion of our souls, re-joining from past lives.

The next morning, I receive a text message from Mum.

"Are you ready for breakfast?"

"Yes, just bring it on!"

I must confess that this was part of a Cane plan, secretly forged on the night before Ju-long arrived. Actually, it was my Mum's idea to give Ju-long money to start a new life with us. He wouldn't just have taken some money but by surprising him, we hope he won't refuse it.

"I'll take care of breakfast," I shout to Ju-long, who is still in the bathroom.

Shortly after, Ju-long comes out, wearing jeans and a tight T-shirt, shining like an angel.

"What's there for breakfast? I hope there's plenty because I'm SO hungry!"

"I know you used a lot of energy last night but, at the same time, you almost ate me up, so that should kind of balance it out!"

Kiss, kiss; ding, dong.

"Oh, that must be the breakfast; please open," I say.

Of course, my parents have a pass-key to the building and my flat, so they are standing outside my front door.

"Mrs And Mr Cane, what a surprise! Come in!"

Mum gives him a warm hug, "Yes, we're a hugging family. You should know that by now. And very informal, I may add."

"Let me take the bags, Dad."

Dad IS a man of plenty, just not regarding body fat. Not that he was afraid that there would not be enough food, but to ensure there is much to choose from. Here are even oranges for my juicer.

Loong pops in with a comment. "Carl intuitively knows that life IS full of possibilities, possible choices… and wealth. It is something Ju-long must bring into his consciousness."

"Welcome to the UK, Ju-long." A handshake and a hug - the men's way.

Soon we are sitting around the dining table, enjoying an excellent breakfast. I catch Mum's eye. She gives me a subtle nod. She is waiting for the right moment.

"It is a tradition in our family…"

Nice move, Mum. He is not likely to go against a family tradition.

"…to bring something when visiting a home for the first time, especially a new home. Carl gave your grandparents a small altar for the dragon spirit in their new home…"

Now he will expect a small thing; brilliant!

"…and we give you an equally small thing for your first home."

She hands him a small present in the shape of a cube, about three inches.

"Thanks; I wonder what it could be?"

He opens the box. First, there is a card shaped like a heart, reading "Welcome to the UK!" and then a credit card, one of the golden ones, of course. Clever, then he cannot see the amount, and would not dare to ask!

"Well, thank you very much. I surely can use help to get some things for my flat. It's our plan to take a look around to see if there is something suitable. Thank you."

And Loong with another comment: "He must learn to receive gifts as something natural and something he deserves."

He gets up and gives first Mum and then Dad a hug. He is very moved. To get the conversation going again, I turn to Dad.

"Yesterday we spoke to Mrs Yu on the computer. Do you think it's possible for Ju-long's grandparents to get a video communication connection like their daughter?"

"The retirement home has this as a point on their list. They'll make a place with some computers with communication capabilities for all residents, ministered by and paid for by the retirement home.

I'll try to speed it up a little."

Later, Dad tells me that a small donation has speeded up the plan, and the practical work is in motion.

Mum shoves back the chair. "It is lovely to welcome you to this country. You have your plans, and we have ours as well."

As Mum turns to me, she raises an eyebrow; all happened according to her plan. Again some hugs, and they were on their way. Another check mark on my plan for the day.

The Way of Choosing

Ju-long and I are spending a good portion of the day shopping. At first he is very observant on the price of things, but I talk about quality.

Loong is, as he did yesterday, guiding me according to Ju-long's understanding of life, to harmonise our connection. "If you want something of lesser value because of other qualities, like the colours or shape, it's fine. Just be sure that's why you are choosing it."

At the computer store, Ju-long is looking for a computer suitable for his programming.

"I think this one is good enough for my programming work."

Loong comments on that. "If you settle for 'just enough', you'll always end up with just enough in your life. Just enough pay, just enough housing, even love. A person with low self-worth will settle for just enough, or even 'hardly enough'. That is not a way to live - it's just survival!"

I do my best to follow Loong's guidance. "Do you dare to buy a big, stupendous computer - one for programming, gaming, video, 3D and everything?"

It takes some time for him to find the courage to choose a powerful computer, but then he starts again with the monitor, the display - the same 'good enough' thing.

"What is the BEST monitor in the shop? Is even that good enough?"

"You're really pushing me today, Luzi!"

"It's about you getting the difference between surviving and living! I'm pushing you, maybe even over the cliff. You may doubt yourself, but I know that you trust in me. I trust in me! You think I'm rich because I have a wealthy father, and you think Carl is rich because he is smart! Dad is not so smart in that sense, he has just found the Holy Grail, so to speak. He intuitively knows how the world and life work and how to act on it."

"But Luzi, you must agree that one needs to have money to be able to spend money."

"Sorry to disappoint you on that one. You must KNOW without a shadow of a doubt that the money will be there when you have need of it. That's the way Dad lives his life. I know it must be hard to have so much trust in life. Sadly, it works the same way if you KNOW that you must work hard to earn money, to get a flat, or to get a scholarship."

"I got the flat because your dad pulled some strings."

"That is not the point here. The point is that it WAS EASY. Let's look at the synchronicity from MY perspective. Something led me to the love of my life - you - but we can talk about that later. Then you got the work permit, then your grandparents moved to relieve your mother, and now you're here in London; with me. That's MY CREATION, MY LIFE. –

And it's not a mind thing. I can't think, wish, want, focus or demand it, but I can feel, deep in my heart, that this is what my life should be about."

I can see that Ju-long is starting to fade away, so I change the subject.

"Let's leave it for now and find a nice monitor fit to partner your computer."

Ju-long is walking around, now looking at specifications and not (so much) at price tags.

"I think it could be this one. It works for programming, gaming and video."

"But do you FEEL it is this one?"

"Well, yeah."

"OK, then it's this one; but why just ONE monitor, dear? I've seen programmers and gamers using two, and even three! I know it's frightening; I can FEEL your fear."

"But I don't know where this fear is coming from; it doesn't make any sense. There's nothing to be afraid of!"

"But there is; in your memory… You know that I can be strange, or stranger, at times… but if there's no reason in this life, it must come from somewhere else. We'll talk about it at some other time, too but, for now, you may settle for any number of monitors that you feel acceptable."

Ju-long wants to please me, so he chooses two monitors.

"Are you happy now?"

"Yes, I'm very pleased with you, AND I LOVE YOU WHATEVER YOU CHOOSE!"

During this talk, I felt that it was more than me speaking the words. Loong smiles at me. "We were a whole choir, but we are here just to guide the truth out of your heart."

There is space enough for the computer, monitors and other things in the car but, as we keep shopping, furniture, carpets and other larger things will be delivered later in the afternoon.

On the way home we stop to get some takeaway food. We have both worked up quite an appetite during our shopping efforts, and are now looking forward to a great meal and a bottle of wine.

Ju-long's things have arrived and are now in his flat, but we are too exhausted to deal with it today. We are now cuddling together under some blankets watching a movie, drinking some more wine. I have even managed to find some nuts and dried fruit in the kitchen.

"Ju-long?"

"Yes?"

"I love you, no matter what you choose. You know that, don't you?"

"Yes, I know that. I may not know to choose the best computer, but that I know; that I feel."

"Yes, you KNOW and you FEEL. That's what I was talking about today. Now I feel for some more wine. Will you do that for me?"

"Anything."

"And you know what? I KNOW that you have to sleep in my bed tonight because yours is in a card box in one hundred pieces!"

"I KNOW that too!"

Britannia

The next morning I have paved the way for some job interviews, and now Ju-long is just about to be on his way, a little nervous but, at the same time, excited. With my arms around him, I look him in the eyes.

"With the love in your heart that you feel for me, you'll find a job in London. And remember: don't look for a job, or search for a job, just FIND a job!"

"And that's not the same thing?"

"NO! Feel into it. When you look and search, you're in doubt, and you create the event of looking or searching. When you start your quest to FIND a job, then it's an adventure! Then you can see yourself standing in front of the opportunity of this job, and you just have to choose it! It's out there as a possibility, already created."

"So instead of creating an event where I'm searching, I create an event where I have found a job."

"Yes, dear; now go out and find the job you've already created."

I kiss him and send him on his way before I take the subway to the university. While I am sitting on the train my nose starts to tickle, and I sneeze. Then I realise that it is Loong.

"I think he's beginning to get it. Now he must realise that it's not a mental thing; I mean the creation part. The job is already there; now it's just about synchronicity, where his human part will meet it."

"I see the creations as bubbles of possibilities, where some are closer to us, energetically, than others."

"Yes, it's a good picture for the mind, Luzi."

"I hope we didn't scare him too much, Loong?"

"We gave him a hard time yesterday, but it helps the energies to fall into place for what he's doing today."

Just before teatime, I get a text from Ju-long.

"I have a job! See you back home!"

"Then let us go out for dinner tonight!"

On my way home, I buy a red rose for Ju-long. Back on the block, I knock on his door. He opens it, standing in some nice outfit.

"Ta-ra! I've been shopping, and the card didn't even run empty."

"What a handsome man I'll be dining with tonight. A rose for you, and congratulations, dear Ju-long!"

"Thanks a lot. The day has been SO strange. I had two interviews. They went well, but somehow it didn't feel quite right. They said they would con-tact me later this week. Then I went to the British Library in Euston Road and even before I got inside it felt right! I met your contact, Jean, a very sweet girl, and it so happened that all the right persons were at work and had just ended a meeting; they hadn't even left the room yet. We had tea, and I had a really good time; they were all very nice. There is still all the paperwork and stuff, and there is a LOT to learn. I must even attend some courses. It was just amazing!"

"It is synchronicity at its best."

"I have, of course, informed the two other libraries that I have got a job."

"It's very close to the university library, the Senate House Library that I usually use."

Ju-long is very excited about the new job and cannot wait to get started.

"Did you know that they have more than 100,000 pieces of Chinese literature, and even a large conservation room?"

"No, I didn't; it's really a lot. But what I do know is that I want to change and get something to eat - are you coming?"

"Yes, yes. I'm completely ready for you!"

"I suppose that you've told your family?"

"Yes! And your parents as well - they need to know that their 'investment' has borne fruit, so to speak."

At my place we have a little 'reunion' before I take a

shower and get ready for our celebration dinner in town. Ju-long has asked around to get help to select a nice place for us to dine.

We are now on our way, but I can't get much out of him.

"I decided to find a place with British food, without it getting too heavy, and maybe wine from British grapes. I know that you can get that in Hong Kong as well, but…"

"You want to honour this country by making this choice, and that's very sweet of you. I'm very pleased with that thought, dear."

I feel a bow and gratitude from a majestic being, presenting herself as The Overseer of the Isles. I am very touched.

"I don't expect or demand any worship, but it's nice to be recognised, even though he doesn't know that there actually IS a receiver for his wish to show gratitude for being here."

We have a wonderful evening, although I no longer recall what food we chose, but the wine was fine… and plentiful!

Ju-long just tells me that we had lamb, potatoes, root vegetables and some salad. He can't remember the dessert. "I had too much wine," he says!

Back in my flat we likewise have a wonderful night. We even manage to get a few hours of sleep before we go to work. I have to be away all day and will be home quite late. It gives Ju-long some time to 'land' and to arrange his things in the flat. For some reason, his bed is still in its box.

Elvendale City

Ju-long has been with me in London for almost three months now, and it is wonderful. When not at work, we are together most of the time. We both have some work we can do at home; I have the most. We realise that it works best if we each work alone in our own flat. Otherwise we distract each other.

As easy as it was for Ju-long to get a job at the library, as difficult it seems to be for him to get a scholarship he wants. I can feel how frustrated he is about the scholarship, so I have decided to visit Elvendale, something I have not done since Ju-long arrived. I lie down on my bed, as I did the first time I got in contact with Elvendale, and look up at the ceiling. I am not tired, but I suddenly feel drowsy and close my eyes.

First comes the smell of grass and dirt, and then the unmistakable smell of Josela's perfume. I open my eyes and realise that I'm closer to the city than ever before, but still out on the grassy plains. Close by, Josela is sitting on a beautiful blanket.

"Greetings, Luzi - how about a glass of cold, white wine to distract your feelings?"

"Hello, Josela. That would be nice!"

Josela pours a glass of sparkling white wine and hands it to me. I sniff in the scent; flowers, a hint of honey… and is it cinnamon? I take a sip; cold, fresh and not too sweet.

"It's very lovely, Josela!"

"I've made it myself."

"How do you do that?"

"I just imagine how it would taste and feel, and then it's there. I think the cinnamon is my perfume, or it could be the wine; I mean, I've created it, and it's 'my' smell."

I take another sip of the wine.

"I wish that I could be here all the time!"

"Well, in a sense you are; you're just not aware of it. You're caught up in the life on Earth, and that's the way it should be. When you KNOW it's the time, you'll be in both realms."

"It seems that we, I mean Ju-long and I, are caught up in a dead end."

"You're troubled because Ju-long strives so hard to get a scholarship. Neither of you can see the whole picture; that's why you're worried. It has to do with synchronicity, or timing, as you might say. Talk to him again about synchronicity and how it worked with his job. You must both trust in your creative abilities and relax into knowing that things will work out fine."

"So we must wait until the synchronicity is right?"

"No; you must trust in the synchronicity, but without putting your focus on WAITING or you may be waiting forever, since that's where your creative energy will go."

"Yes of course; silly me!"

I look at the city in the distance, built in layers on a low mountain peak with a long bridge supported by stone pillars leading to it from the grassy plains over the valley and the river.

"I've never visited the city; can we go there?"

"It'll be easier just to BE there, but walking here in Elvendale is much faster than on your physical planet, so come on!"

We glide towards the start of the bridge as if we were walking on one of those rolling sidewalks seen mostly in airports. It is totally without effort. When we arrive at the first gate leading onto the bridge to the city, I see Loong next to it, seemingly sleeping. Now he raises his head.

"Oh, I've woken the dragon!"

I feel Loong smiling.

"We never sleep in Elvendale. Well, we do not NEED to sleep or rest. I was just lying down, enjoying the warmth of our star shining on my fur."

Both Josela and I hug the big, fluffy dragon, and he starts to purr like a cat.

"I've never been in Elvendale City before, so Josela is showing me around."

Loong stretches his wings and folds them back tight to the body.

"Then I suggest that you get a view from above before diving into the streets. Get on my back, both of you, and get a firm grip on my fur. It's totally safe - no one falls and dies here unless they choose to."

I am in the front and Josela is behind me. Loong takes off with a glide; he doesn't need to flap his wings. As we circle upwards for a better view, I notice some smoke coming out of a volcano on the mountain range next to the mountain hosting the city.

"Is the city in danger from the volcano?"

"Oh no," Josela says, smiling, "It's just a theatrical effect, or you could say that we're just letting off some steam!"

Loong circles higher, and soon I have a view of a vast landscape with mountains, fields, forests, valleys and, far off, a sea. Streams are running into a river which floats into a large lake below the city's mountain. Here, there is a harbour with all kinds of ships and boats. None of them have smelly or smoking engines. On the other side of the lake, a river flows to the sea.

We are now circling above the city itself. The walls of the houses are shining white in the sunlight. Some of the roofs remind me of traditional Chinese houses, others are domes, of which some seem to be of glass. Everything looks beautiful and clean. Loong descends, and I can see a circular place below us. It is white like the city, and decorated with patterns in different colours. When we land, Loong shrinks to the size of a cat, and soon a lovely Birman cat is walking in front of us, showing the way with his tail right up in the air.

We have landed in the lower part of the city, now we are walking towards the periphery of the round place where a street leads to the upper part. There are some shops and workshops.

"Why are people working to make things, when they could just create them in an instant?"

"It's their passion. Creating a thing in an instant is like you buying something instead of making it yourself. If you have a passion for crafting something, it will give you much joy in the process and much satisfaction when you stand with the final product. It's an entirely different experience."

"So have you made your own clothes?"

"Yes, dear, even the shoes!"

"It's easier with fur; you don't have to make anything," Loong comments.

"Another thing, Loong - does anyone eat meat?"

"Well, someone could, by creating a steak, but to kill an animal for the meat would be unthinkable. I don't think anyone eats meat, though; it simply wouldn't benefit you in the energies we live in."

"How about waste?"

"There is no waste. We don't even have toilets! Things that are no longer in use will return to the basic or dormant energy."

"I could ask and ask forever, but how do the Sidhe prepare for the physical life on Earth?"

Loong stops, turns around and looks me straight in the eyes. I can feel he's up to something and he enjoys it.

"There are many non-physical training grounds like Earth. A part of your consciousness even teaches there!"

"What?!"

"Oh, yes. Do you think you are wasting all the time that your person is sleeping?"

There is definitely much more to life than I thought just a few months ago; even a few hours ago. Now I can see a lot of stairs in front of us and turn to Josela.

"Wouldn't it have been smarter to build the city down on the plains? Then you wouldn't need all those stairs."

"We GLIDE the stairs, not walk, just as we glided towards the bridge. A town on a flat terrain isn't as charming as this one that grows up the mountainside so town and mountain become one."

We ascend through layers and layers of beautiful houses with all kinds of purposes and looks, many different colours and features. I learn that stairs spiral up the mountains and, at the same time, other stairs take short cuts and go straight to the top. We take the spiral to get the maximum experience, and I must say it is a very impressive journey to the mountain-top. Here lies a large tower that serves as 'The Grand Hall' for meetings of many kinds. I turn my back to the tower to get a look outside the city. At the top level of the city, I am closer to the ground than when we flew over it with Loong. I clearly see fields and orchards, and some farms. The fields have an untouched spot of nature in between, as well as ponds and small streams with bridges. Everything is lush. It looks like a patchwork.

Again, I turn to Josela. "Why would you choose to incarnate on Earth, when it's much more difficult in every way to live there?"

"It's the physical life that is the ultimate experience. It's not about easy or difficult; it's about the full experience of life."

I have a very good time with Loong and Josela and now, turning my focus back to my human life, I feel much lighter and with great confidence that everything is in its best order.

A New Home

This weekend Ju-long and I have arranged to visit Mum and Dad in their lovely home.

We arrive at around ten in the morning, early enough to spend some time in their wonderful garden, before we all lend a hand in the preparation of lunch. It is a tradition in our family to share the preparation as well as the meal itself, to bring us closer to each other.

While I am working in the kitchen Loong makes himself present, and I can see him sitting in his cat form on the kitchen bench.

"It's much like when you prepare the key points with the key players in your lives before incarnating."

"I didn't think life was predestined?"

"It's not a predestined plan, but a guideline you could follow to achieve the goals you've set up to accomplish. You can always change direction and make different choices. That's the free will part. Remember that there are many paths to the same goal!"

"Why do I see people make so many rotten choices in their life?"

"Many, or dare I say, most people, do not make these planning sessions, but simply return into the same energies, bloodline and karma that they left when they died."

"Can it be that I've felt some of these points in my life? It's like being more aware of a situation, 'feeling' that something special happens."

"Oh, yes. And there have been some lately, right? That's why you must be so still in your mind that you can feel or sense what direction you must take to get to the nearest point, that's sitting 'out there' as a beacon to attract you. If it has to do with other people, there has to be synchronicity as well."

While dining, we talk about how things are going in Hong Kong. It seems that both Ju-long's and my grandparents are doing fine, and they have started to spend more time together. At some point, we are all happy about that because my grandparents are not able to take care of themselves. Hopefully they feel content about moving into the retirement home. Dad has arranged that there will be room for them when the time comes. Ju-long's mother has become much happier and has taken up some old connections, and even gained some new friends.

We do not see my sister, Anna, very much. She is either studying or travelling, but we keep a close connection.

After lunch, we are in the garden. I bring up a subject that Ju-long and I have been discussing for a little while.

"We've been talking about moving to the country. Even though we both have our jobs and other activities in London, in the city, we should be able to keep them. I feel more drawn to nature lately, and the connection gives me much harmony in an otherwise hectic working life."

Mum looks excited, which she always does when something new comes up. "It sounds like a splendid idea. Do you have any areas in mind?"

"No, I think we must wait until Ju-long gets his scholarship, so we don't have too many jokers in play."

"Or it may be the other way around. That you find some place to live and then the scholarship will present itself."

Dad, who is always the helping angel, offers to help. "I'll look into the scholarship thing. I do not understand why it should be such a big issue."

"Thanks Dad; that would be great."

Loong, who is sitting at the edge of the lawn under some flowering bushes, turns my attention to a broader spectrum. "Can you feel the energies loosen up?"

"Yes, I feel quite excited already; how strange."

"Your mother hit it straight on. It's about synchronicity, where all the parts must be in motion at the same time - throw all the jokers into the game!"

Back at Ju-long's place we are looking on the Internet for some suitable places where we would like to live. Ju-long has drifted off while I am busy at his computer. Now he poses a question, trying to narrow our search. "Why not by the sea, like in Hong Kong, or is that too far from London?"

"Well, I guess not. The east coast is not that far away, if the connection by train is manageable."

My phone rings; it is Dad.

"Hi, Luzi; I've been looking into the scholarship thing for Ju-long and, for some strange reason, Brighton keeps popping up. It's not close to London, but actually by the Channel. I'll send you a link so you can check it out. Mum sends her best wishes."

"You wouldn't believe it, Dad. Ju-long has just asked me why our new home could not be by the sea, like in Hong Kong!"

"Well, you check it out and let us know what you find out."

"We will. Thanks, Dad. Say hello to Mum. I love you!"

After that, things really move fast. The University of Brighton is situated, as Dad said, on the south coast of England. We have found a lovely house to rent just outside the city. When Ju-long moved to England we thought that HE would have to travel to study, and now it is ME who must go to London. Luckily, I can do much of my work via the Internet.

The next morning, when Ju-long has left for work, I fade off to Elvendale, meeting Josela at the round city place where we are sitting in the shade under a large tree, drinking cherry juice out of large glasses.

"I can't see why there wasn't any scholarship for Ju-long in London. There should be plenty."

Josela brings forth her wisdom. "Oh, but there are a lot of scholarship opportunities in and around London. It just didn't fit with your plans to move out into the country. There is no reason to WAIT with one wish if you can do it all at once. You can see now that the synchronicity works far better than your mind can plan!"

"But he got the scholarship first, and then we started to look for a place to live; or was it the other way around?"

"That's just the way you see it, because you are used to functioning in a linear timeline. Things will be much easier when you get out of your linear thinking, outside of your mind. When you started to focus on a new place to live, the jokers were all put on the table, and the synchronicity could take action."

We run into emotional as well as practical chaos the day before we are moving to our new home in Brighton, because Ju-long's grandmother dies.

Ju-long must leave for Hong Kong to take care of everything and comfort his mother and grandfather, while I have to deal with moving to Brighton.

The removal men arrive early the next morning to clear out our flats, where all things have already been packed and ready for loading. Ju-long has been up even earlier, so he can get on his plane to Hong Kong. Neither Ju-long nor I have had any sleep during the short night, and I feel woozy and out of focus.

I am longing so much for a good, strong cup of coffee, but Loong advises against it, telling me that the freshness I would feel in the beginning would turn on me later, when I would be driving, with a very low energy. He recommends that I drink a lot of water, both now and while driving. It will keep my system awake and my senses alert.

"Sit down for a few moments and visit Elvendale. Here you can relax and maybe take a short nap."

I sit down and close my eyes. For a short while I can hear the men moving around in the flat, but then the song of the birds in Elvendale drowns out their noise. I can feel Loong's furry body and don't even bother opening my eyes. I just tuck myself into him and fall into a blissful sleep.

I wake what feels like hours later, giving thanks to Loong for having been my cuddly toy, before I turn my focus back to my flat in London. I look at my watch and realise that only a few moments have passed. Now I feel fully rested and go to check on Ju-long's flat.

Shortly before noon we are ready to leave for Brighton, but I invite the men to a casual lunch at one of my favourite cafés nearby, before we head south.

About three hours later, we arrive in Brighton. I already have the keys to the house, but the owner shows up anyway to welcome me. She had expected to see both Ju-long and me, so I briefly explain the situation.

She is a small woman, a little plump, and with curly, grey hair. She is nicely dressed in blue shirt and a skirt, with a white silk scarf around her neck. She wears black shoes with some heels. She is driving a small, but expensive car.

I have arranged some of our things in our new home, but want to wait until Ju-long comes back so we can do it together. While Ju-long is gone, I have also been checking out some new job opportunities closer to Brighton. Now I have a job at the University of Kent, Tonbridge Centre, a little more than one hour by train. It will primarily be about teaching literature and writing. I will keep my jobs in London. I have been contacting the friends who have helped me gather the information for the book, and we have updated each other on the latest news in our lives. Ling in Beijing, who introduced me to the Chinese Sidhe, has spent much time at the excavations in Xinjiang with her students. Lately, she has been working hard with the students' papers as part of their examination requirements. Now she is putting the final touches to her own science report. Josephine, who got me to chase dragons, and her husband, Ping, in Shanghai, are still enjoying each other and their respective jobs at the publisher and the zoo.

Ju-long returns to Brighton, and we are enjoying making the house ours, as well as enjoying each other. Ju-long is still doing some work for the British Library, but most of his time is spent at the local university teaching and being taught. Mum, Dad and Anna have been visiting us, and they are all very excited about our new home, both the inside of the house and the garden and the surroundings, especially nature. The house itself is of uneven sandstones, so they differ in both size and colour. It has two floors, plus a cellar under a part of it. The roof is 45 degrees and covered with slate tiles. The garden is kept semi-wild, with a lot of herbaceous perennials and bushes, while the open areas are grass. There are mostly large, flat stones laid out as stepping-stones in the lawns. Part of the garden has a shallow wall and an arch to the fields behind the house. There is a small vegetable garden as well, where Ju-long is spending quite some time. Here he really relaxes.

Ju-long in Elvendale

A month later, as Ju-long and I have just started to manage ourselves in our new lives, Ju-long's grandfather dies. We both go to Hong Kong to take care of this situation. We get a three-month visa for Ju-long's mother, whose name is Ting, and she returns with us for a kind of vacation, to put some distance from the recent events of her son leaving for England and the loss of her parents. We have some in-depth talks, she and I. At times, she feels very alone and sad, but we manage to bring some clarity and optimism into her life. When she goes back to Hong Kong, to the flat and her job at the mall, I feel confident that she will be able to move on with her life.

One afternoon, Ting and I are sitting in the garden under an old tree, sipping hot tea out of two large mugs. I can instantly feel a large number of visitors coming to the place. They can feel the despair and, at the same time, the hope, and some of them can tap into the possibilities in life in front of Ting. Loong calls me to Elvendale, so my consciousness expands to be there as well and, from a little distance, I can see Ting and myself sitting on the wooden chairs under the tree. The salver is on the wooden table between us. From this place of awareness I can see all the entities that sit around us, and everything is so beautiful and full of compassion. I am so moved that I get tears in my eyes, both physically and non-physically, if one can say that.

Loong speaks to me in his silent voice. "Her name, Ting, means enduring. Not that she should endure pain and suffering all her life, but to indicate that she will come through the tough times. Right now, she feels that life works against her, but everything works to free her from the suffering that she feels she's in right now and has been in for a long time."

My talk with Loong is instant, meaning that it does not take any time to complete. It is like dumping a package of knowingness into my awareness. I instantly know all he says. It means that Loong and I can have a conversation at the same time as I speak with Ting. If it has been thought through the brain, it will have taken both time and focus, because that is the way the brain functions.

"You're crying, dear Luzi!"

"Oh no, Ting, I have tears in my eyes, but it's because I can feel all the entities that are around us, sitting compassionately close by and providing healing."

Ting gets tears in her eyes as well. "It's probably a good thing to cry a little."

"Or a lot," Loong relays through me.

"Do you think I can feel them as well?"

"Oh yes, certainly; just say hello in your thoughts and give them an imaginary hug, and you'll feel them hugging you back."

Ting starts to cry uncontrollably, and her body is

shaking. After some time, she's able to speak.

"I really felt the hug, and it was so beautiful. Can you see the creatures too?"

"Yes, but not as you would see them in this world; I mostly see their souls, so to speak, their colours."

"Oh, their auras!"

"Well, not exactly. When people see auras, they usually see an extension of a body's energy field and thought patterns, which include emotions and what's unconscious. What I see is what they are at the moment - their consciousness, if you like."

"In China, we believe in dragons, as you well know. I don't suppose you have dragons in England."

"But we do. Dragons are not bound to any physical place. Right next to us, my friend Loong is dwelling. He's a mighty, white dragon, mostly covered in fur. I met him in Shanghai, where he lives in the physical realm as a white, Birman cat."

While I am writing this, Loong drops a comment.

"One does not have to believe in dragons to feel the hug. One has to open the heart to send out the love that the hug contains. The open heart will then sense the hug that returns. It is the power of the hug; it opens the heart."

"Loong tells me that he'll be there whenever you need a hug, or someone to talk to."

"Tell him that I'm very grateful!"

"You just told him yourself! You don't need me to be a middleman. And he'll ALWAYS hear you. It's the great thing about not having physical ears, he says with a big smile on his furry face."

Ting starts to laugh. She sees Loong's grinning face with her inner eyes, and I can hear him laughing outrageously loud, so probably everyone in Elvendale can hear him.

"Joy, my friend, is SO important," he says. At that moment, I feel a laugh coming up from my tummy and now Ting, I, and all the rest around us have a good laugh.

"See, this clears things out," Loong says and, from my Elvendale view, I see that the energies around Ting change into lighter colours. He tickles my face with his fur and I, sitting beside Ting, come out with a huge sneeze. I start laughing again, and so does the rest of the group.

It is a lovely afternoon and, at the dining table in the evening, I see life tingling in Ting's eyes. Her soul has returned into her life because her heart has invited it in.

Later, when I am alone with Ju-long, he asks me what had happened during my talk with his mother. I reply that she has to tell him herself. This way, she is forced to put words to her feelings, as well as giving both mother and son the opportunity to talk about feelings on a deeper level than they are used to.

Now that we are in bed, Ju-long tells me about his talk with his mother.

"Mum was very excited about what happened in the garden this afternoon. She said that at first she felt a little silly talking about faeries and dragons but, shortly after, she was relaxed and peaceful. Mum has changed a lot. She's much more as she was when I was a kid. It is as if a heavy blanket has gone from over her head."

"The blanket is a good picture of the feelings that have held her life energy at bay, woven from all her feelings and judgements."

"I thought that faeries and dragons were only in your book?"

"It seems that your woman is even weirder than you, though. It must be time for you to learn the deeper truth of what is happening in my life."

I start to tell Ju-long the condensed story that I would have told him so many times before, but had not found the right moment for it.

Just before I finish my story Ju-long fades off, and we are lying on our backs, hand in hand, on the small mound as I did the first time I visited Elvendale. Josela is there to greet us.

"Welcome to Elvendale, both of you. I am Josela, the 'welcome-bidder' of Elvendale. It sounds better than the gatekeeper. Finally we meet, Ju-long."

"Is this one of Luzi's dreams?"

"Dreams may not be what you thought them to be. Our consciousness is simply meeting outside your normal awakening state. There is nothing mysterious about it. In these meetings you'll have full control, not like in most dreams, where the dream controls you."

We sit up. I keep Ju-long's hand in mine, making him feel safe.

"It's all right, dear. I was pretty disoriented myself when I came here the first time. I hope that Loong will show up."

"You mean the white dragon you've told me about?"

"He just appears as a dragon or a cat. He isn't even a he or a she, but I think we should save that part for another time."

I hear Loong calling from inside the forest.

"Helloooo?"

"Here he comes, and there's nothing to fear."

Ju-long looks at the edge of the forest where we can now hear a large creature brushing through the vegetation.

Loong now comes out into the clearing at a slow pace, and Josela is running towards him to show Ju-long that there is nothing to fear.

"Come here and get a hug, you big fur-ball."

They come to us, and Loong sends us an inner smile.

"Welcome to Elvendale, Ju-long. I have looked forward to meeting you. I do not so much shake hands, but I'm quite good at hugging, especially receiving them."

He gives yet another smile, and now Ju-long and I slowly walk up to him. I touch him on the neck, and I lead Ju-long's hand to the same spot.

"Hello, Loong. It is nice to meet you, although it feels very strange and so real."

Loong laughs.

"It IS real. Life is real, dreams are real, and con-sciousness meeting in creation is most certainly real."

I can feel Ju-long struggling as his human intellect tries to validate the truth of this experience. I let us stay for a short while before we say goodbye and withdraw to the human realm. I do not wake up Ju-long, but let him slip into his normal dream world. We will talk about this experience tomorrow.

The next morning, while still in bed, Ju-long and I talk about his first visit to Elvendale. I start out by asking if he remembers being in Elvendale.

"So it IS real! I really talked to a dragon!"

"The most exciting thing is that he IS a dragon, he IS a cat, AND he IS whatever he chooses to be!"

"So I can choose to be a dragon? I don't think so, no matter how hard I try!"

"You're right. The HUMAN part of you can't, but YOU, consciousness, can choose it. Right now, you've chosen to live through numerous lives as a human being."

"You're putting me to the ultimate test here!"

"Don't let your mind come between us. I feel that we shouldn't get too much into this right now. Let it sink into you, and we'll continue at a later time."

"You're right. Let's get up and have some breakfast; I could eat a dragon, with fur and all!"

We have breakfast with Ting, Ju-long's mother, while we make a loose plan for the day.

Synchronicity

What is the chance of meeting the 'right' Chinese man, who is living on Hong Kong Island, in a middle-sized city in the southern part of England? Well, pretty slim I would say, but that was what happened to Ting! It should, if anything, tell her about synchronicity!

Ting has asked if she could make dinner for us this evening, to contribute to the household. Still new to most shopping places in Brighton, we decide to try one of the Chinese groceries out, since Ting wants to make something Chinese.

We are now cruising round the store, and I see Ting talking to an Asian-looking gentleman walking around with a notepad and checking the shelves. Now they laugh, and Ting looks a little embarrassed. They keep talking as if they knew each other. After a short while, Ting waves us over.

"This is Mr Fan. He lives on Hong Kong Island. Can you believe it?"

Ju-long and I say hello. I think we are both wondering why Ting and Mr Fan are so informal in both speech and body language. He has an average body, has friendly eyes and an inviting smile.

Ting laughs a little.

"I thought he was the owner, since he's checking the shelves, but he's a travelling salesman."

"Yes, I have many customers in the UK and about thirty in Brighton alone."

I wonder why a man living in China is checking shelves in the UK.

"Mr Fan, do you really have to travel to the UK to sell Chinese products?"

"It is not necessary, but I like to be face-to-face with my clients so, a few times a year, I take 'the grand tour', as I call it, meeting the clients and presenting new goods."

"It's like my dad. He says that the face-to-face meeting makes all the difference. He's English, by the way; my mum is Chinese."

I can see that Mr Fan is thinking for a short moment. Then he presents a proposal.

"I would very much like, if you have the time, of course, to show you some of my finest things. The chef is preparing samples in the restaurant upstairs."

Ting responds promptly.

"That would be lovely. We do have the time, right?"

"Yes, of course," I reply. Ju-long and I are signalling to each other with the eyes.

A few minutes later, Ting and Mr Fan vanish in each other's company, and Ju-long and I observe them from a little distance. Now their dialogue stops, and it is easy to see that they gaze deep into each other's eyes. It is a deep connection, a reconnection beyond time and age. It is the ageless soul. I whisper to Ju-long.

"It's a reunion. They have known each other in another life, and they're now starting to recall some deep feelings from that life, or maybe even lives."

"They're acting quite peculiar. Well, you're right, like old friends. As you know, this is not normal behaviour in China."

I slowly walk over to the two, addressing Mr Fan.

"Mr Fan, if you are not occupied elsewhere, Ju-long and I would like to invite you to dinner tonight."

"It would bring me great joy to be with you all this evening. I have a lot to attend to, so it would suit me fine if I could arrive around eight?"

"Eight would be fine, wouldn't you think, Ting?"

"Oh yes! But we have to hurry back. I have a lot to do!"

Ju-long smiles; I can see that he enjoys seeing his mum with so much energy.

"Don't worry, Mum. Luzi and I will be your keen servants."

After completing the shopping we leave Mr Fan with the address, directions and a phone number. Life has just taken a whole new and unexpected turn for Ting.

We spend the rest of the day cooking, interrupted only by quick meals, and then Ju-long and I go for a walk to give Ting some time on her own. Ju-long voices his worries.

"Mum looks so happy, but we do not know anything about Mr Fan. I would hate to see her disappointed."

"You must trust in the synchronicity of this. It's already at work, or else the two wouldn't have met. You must relax and enjoy seeing your mother so alive. Don't place worries into the situation."

Mr Fan arrives shortly before eight, all dressed up and in a great mood. Ting and I are making the last preparations, so Ju-long opens the door.

"Mr Fan, welcome. Come in, here's a hanger for your coat."

"Hello, Mr Wang; I'm happy to be here."

From the dining room, I see that Mr Fan has his hands full of flowers and chocolate, so I join the two in the hall.

"Welcome, Mr Fan."

"Hello, Ms Cane. The chocolate is for you and Mr Wang and the flowers are for the cook."

"Thank you so much. Let me take the flowers as well, so you can get out of your coat."

"Thank you, Ms Cane. What a lovely house."

Ting comes out, and I hand over the flowers to Mr Fan.

"For the one who has provided this house with such a wonderful smell!"

"Oh, thank you so much. They're lovely."

I decide to cut down on the formalities.

"We're not so formal in my family. I'm Luzi, short for Lucia. This is Ju-long and his mother, Ting."

"Oh yes, that suits me perfectly. I am Cheng."

"Does it mean 'travelling'?"

"I would say 'journey'. It fits my current job as a travelling salesman!"

Ting adds with a laugh, "And your last name, Fan, means 'bee', so I assume you're quite busy."

Cheng laughs too. "I sure am a busy traveller."

Ju-long leads us into the dining room, and I find a suitable vase for the flowers, which get a place at the one end of the dining table. The chocolate ends up on the coffee table.

Cheng looks around. "I really would like a tour of this remarkable house later. It seems quite old - historical, I mean."

"It can be dated back to the 1600s. It's a rented house and Joan, the owner, is very helpful."

The evening goes very well, and it is quite late before we bid Cheng goodnight. He turns out to be a very nice man. He has lost his wife, and is now spending all his time on his work, which he perseveringly performs. When he and Ting are both back in Hong Kong, they decide to live together. Ting is now a joint owner in Cheng's business and has thereby got new contentment in her life. At the same time, she has gained new friends, and we can hear how happy they are each time we talk with them both.

I have just been talking with my grandparents, and Grandma tells me that 'our' hotel on the Wah Fu Road has closed, so she recommends The T Hotel on Pok Fu Lam Road. It will be the place where Ju-long and I will stay the next time we visit Hong Kong.

Kuthumi

It is late afternoon, and the disc of the Sun is nearly touching the hills to the north. I'm sitting by the dyke that marks the border between our garden and the fields on the other side, looking at the cattle grazing while two young calves are playing nearby. I hear some swallows in the air, flying close to the animals, pursuing insects to feed to their young. A voice that seems to come from my left steals my attention.

"Namaste! It is I, Kuthumi!"

"Namaste?"

I sense Kuthumi shaking his head.

"No; NAMASTE!!!"

He says it loudly, very joyfully, and in a voice that encourages me to repeat.

"Namaste."

He says it once again, and still in the same voice, to indicate that I do not sound very joyful, so I try again, putting more feeling into it.

"Namaste!"

"It means that I honour the divine in you. It's a Hindu greeting."

"Oh!"

"I formally present myself as Kuthumi lal Singh of Ah-Kir-Rah."

"Greetings, Kuthumi lal Singh of Ah-Kir-Rah."

"Kuthumi lal Singh is the human name I was born with in one lifetime. Ah-Kir-Rah is MY name; my soul name, if you like. It was in that lifetime that Kuthumi came into realisation, or what you call ascended and became a master. It happened here in England, more precisely in Cambridge; at the university."

"You must tell me more about that. I have never met an ascended master before!"

"I'm not here to talk about myself, but about Ju-long's grandparents, to give you a better understanding of what is happening in your life."

"I'll be very grateful to be enlightened about their part in my life, but maybe you can tell me more about yourself later?"

Kuthumi ignores my question and begins explaining the situation to me.

"When Ju-long's grandparents agreed to move to the retirement home, they agreed to changes in their life, and those changes were to let go of clinging to some old habits and move on through death and into new human lives. At the same time, they gave Ting and Ju-long the push to move on in their lives, as well as showing a possibility for your grandparents to live in a nursing home when they can't manage living by themselves in their flat."

"What you're saying is that making a choice on the human level will make things happen on many other levels?"

"What I'm saying is that making a small opening or change on one level may set large changes in motion. That's a good thing. Figuratively, you just have to move a finger to fly to new heights."

"It's about daring to make a choice and bring it into one's life by acting on that choice, I guess."

"Yes, but, depending on the choice, you may not necessarily have to act to bring the possibilities into being, you just have to act when you see or sense the potential."

"Kuthumi, people are making wishes all the time but, most of the time, nothing happens."

"There's a huge difference between a wish and a conscious choice. You can wish for a better life, but you have to consciously choose to change your current life, with all its habits, to bring about those changes. If you don't act differently from yesterday, your tomorrow will be just the same as today, and today will be the same as yesterday."

"The conscious choice runs much deeper than a human wish, right?"

"Yes! Humans make wishes, but consciousness chooses!"

"It must be because humans believe that the solution must come from outside of themselves, being given from an outside force, while consciousness takes full responsibility for its life."

"You're right again, dear Luzi! Now let's celebrate the conscious life and, at the same time, show compassion for the human life."

I feel that Kuthumi grabs my hands, and we start a swirling dance in the great halls of humanity. There are colours and fireworks everywhere, and I see millions of other entities joining us in celebration. The dance lifts the heavy mental energies that have built up around me during our talk.

At some point, we are far out in space and Earth is just a tiny, blue dot far away. I can't SEE that the blue dot is Earth, I just KNOW it. I feel very joyful and light, and Kuthumi comments on that.

"The 'first' feminine attribute is expressive joy, the dancing and the singing. The 'first' masculine attribute is compassion, or what you may call love. Quite the opposite of what is told today, where the masculine is the expression and the female is both love and compassion. One expression has been kept, though, namely the creation of new life, the birth. If you're into colours, then the core feminine colour is indigo or blue, and the masculine is crimson or red."

"Why have the attributes and colours been switched?"

"Well, it's a long story. I'll make it short, but then most of the details will be missing. Before the physical universe existed, the radiated consciousness, which you call the soul, was experiencing life as creative consciousness. At some point it got out of hand, and the activity came almost to a standstill. The female, which had been the driving force, felt that it had failed in conducting life experience, and asked the masculine to take over. In honour and compassion to the female, the masculine took over, and a physical universe was created with the purpose of breaking the standstill. The masculine acted with the feminine attributes of expression and creation but, as you see today, the masculine has become addicted to power and does not have the strength to let go of the first female attributes. Another way of looking at it is that the masculine cannot let go of the commitment to the female. One must keep the promise in honour to the feminine aspect!"

"It seems to me like we're in a deadlock. How can we nip the masculine in the bud, and the feminine as well, to get everything flowing again? Can't you, Saint Germain and all the rest of the masters, do something?"

"We're working in many different ways, but it always comes down to the human, who must do the job of choosing differently to make the changes happen. We're working with you right now as well as with numerous others, in so many ways. For instance, we work with humans in the making of nearly every song and movie, to bring information, in a different form, into the human world and into consciousness. The songs and movies which you're attuned to right now are highly potent for bringing awareness to people. You resonate with the truth placed in these works on many different levels. We love to play and act. You may even recognise me in the Star Wars character, C3PO, the golden robot. On unconscious levels, you're contributing to these works as well!"

"I am? Really?"

"Oh, yes. There are some lyrics, melodies and characters which you feel very close to, simply because they're part of your work. You may not be entirely satisfied with some of the work, but humans can be very stubborn and don't listen. The ruby slippers in the movie, Oz, should have been crimson, but the focus was on gems like the emerald, hence The Emerald City in the same movie. The song Over the Rainbow, also from that movie, has been imbued with special qualities in the performance given by Eva Cassidy."

"So, we're manipulating the world?"

"We're working in the world like anyone else, adding our creations to the whole of humanity, for the most part through humans, since it's the way it should be."

Kuthumi pauses, and I can feel a conclusion coming up.

"We will bring an end to this conversation for this time, but we shall meet again, dear Luzi. Namaste!"

"Namaste!"

When I return my focus back to the sunset, the Sun hasn't got any closer to the hills. No time has passed while my dialogue and trip into space with Kuthumi has happened. I get this thought that we have 'all the time in the world' to raise the consciousness of humanity; it's just the matter of how fast humanity will open up and widen the perception of life. The more open a person is, the more it can perceive and then open even more. The Bible is right in saying, 'To whoever has shall more be given' or something like that. I looked up in New Living Translation and found this: 'To those who listen to my teaching, more understanding will be given, and they will have an abundance of knowledge. But for those who are not listening, even what little understanding they have will be taken away from them.'. If knowledge gives no meaning, one will let the knowledge go.

The Spiral of Life

Ju-long and I have come a long way in expanding our understanding of life. For most people, their daily struggles are all there is. They do not understand that it is just a play on the stage of life. They need to see that they are the author and director of their play and that they can change the set at any time. They have to say "CUT" or "BREAK", make different conscious choices, and then continue the play. If one thinks that suicide is a way off the stage, then one is on the wrong track. It will immediately change things, but one will be reborn with the same patterns, and everything will be even more confused, because now one does not know why one had such an urge to end this life.

Luck is something you choose. Not luck, like in winning the lottery, but to be lucky in feeling lucky. It is the feeling of happiness and love for life and one's great creation. Humans tend to fear the day when luck will run out, and that fear will surely kill the luck.

There is no end, just new beginnings. It is about eternal life anywhere in creation, not just on Earth. There is no 'circle of life' if you choose to get off that dreadful carousel, only the spiral of life, an ever-moving journey from possibility to possibility, from one conscious choice to the next.

My book about elves and other creatures of folklore still needs completion. It has taken a whole different turn from what I initially had expected, and I must approach it from a new angle. Luckily, I have a lot of assistance from my beloved sources, with who I look forward to continuing the work.

I am sitting here on this grass-covered hill with clover in flower, beside Ju-long and with Loong lying behind us. In front of us we have the grasslands, the lake, the bridge to Elvendale City and the city on the mountain itself. Farthest out we have the sea stretching to the horizon, where the sunlight is painting the sky in reddish colours, and soon to set, bringing up an indigo sky, blending into velvet black, filled with bright stars in many colours.

The End

I hope you have enjoyed the book and ask you to take a moment to make a short review on your favourite retailer website.

Thanks in advance, Eriqa Queen.

On the next page, you'll find my short comments about this book.

Author's Comments

The living persons in this novel are mostly ficti-
tious, including Luzi. I came to realise that Luzi's
father is based on my publisher, Erik Istrup. The
glyphs are real, and can be found on the Internet
and elsewhere. The souls of the dragons are real,
and so are the Sidhe. At least one 'dragon' and two
Sidhe are with me during the writing, as well as all
the other entities, like Sekhmet and Imhotep, and I
could not have done it without them. Thank you,
friends. The dialogues and events that Luzi has
with these entities are real too, as they happened to
me, as are the octahedron crystal I found in Egypt.

You cannot connect to other realms if you just BE-
LIEVE you can; you have to KNOW. Listen for
the music, or is it the smell that is your strongest
sense? Or you may just feel you must dance with
joy. When you connect, you know; you'll feel the
love pouring in!

I will not try to hide that the name Eriqa Queen is a
pen name. Writing different genres, may otherwise
confuse the audience because they expect specific
contents from a specific author. Eriqa IS a part of
me, and I am true to that part that you may sense
behind the words or between the lines. The aspects
of other lives play a role as well and often speak
and act through the characters in the book, and this
is ALL me. With about 1,470 incarnations on Earth,
the lifespan of this one is of very little importance.

EQ

Additional stuff

There is so much material that in different ways can trigger your depths and make you remember, so this list is just some small examples.

Books

David Spangler. I have not read his books, but it is said, that he's at the forefront according the Sidhe. The central book title is *"Conversations with the Sidhe"*. www.davidspangler.com

"Act of Consciousness", 2015, Adamus Saint-Germain, www.crimsoncircle.com.

"Live Your Divinity", 2012, Adamus Saint-Germain, www.redwheelweiser.com.

"Masters in the New Energy", Adamus Saint-Germain, 2007, www.crimsoncircle.com.

"There's No Such Place as Far Away", Richard Back, HaperCollins, 1993, (first edition in 1979).

"The Red Lion - The Elixir of Eternal Life", 1997, Maria Szepes, Horus Publishing, Inc., (First published in Hungary in 1946).

"The Findhorn Garden by the Findhorn Community" www.findhorn.org

"The Wild Alliance", Søren Hauge, www.wiseheart.

com and www.sorenhauge.dk

"Out on a limb", Sherley MacLaine

"Camino", Sherley MacLaine

"Jonathan Livingston Seagull", Richard Bach.

"The Lord of the Rings", J. R. R. Tolkien.

Songs

The songs are mostly about the relation between the human and the soul, realising that you are the human AND the consciousness. Some are the soul speaking to the human and a few is about the human journey. You may have to feel into this, to realise the message. Remember that the performer/ writer may not know this connection.

"Aloha, E Komo Mai", Jump5 (Lilo and Stitch song).

"Let it go", Demi Lovato (from "Frozen").

"Lost", Anouk.

"Release Me", 2007, writers: Nils Johan Carlsson Westfelt & Erik Olof Althoff, performer: "Oh Laura".

"Over the Rainbow", performed by Eva Cassidy.

"Everybody Hurts", REM, performed by The Corrs (unplugged)

"No Frontiers" REM, performed by The Corrs (unplugged)

"Would you be happier", The Corrs.

"Guardian Angel", Terry Oldfield.

"When can I see you again", Owl City.

"Just give me a reason", Pink feature Nate Ruess.

"I will follow you into the dark", Death Cab for Cutie (Plans), cover by Daniela Andrade.

"We belong to the sea", Aqua.

"Aquarius", Aqua.

"Cuba Libre", Aqua.

"Goodbye to the circus", Aqua.

"Landslide", Fleetwood Mac.

"Take me walking in the rain", Janis Ian.

"Sometimes when I'm dreaming", performed by Katie Melua.

"Go your own way", Nanna (Rocking Horse)

"Leather and Lace", Stevie Nicks (Bella Donna)

"I sing for the things", Stevie Nicks (Rock a little)

"Have anyone ever written anything for you?", Stevie Nicks (Rock a little).

"Soak up the Sun", Sheryl Crow.

"Dream Operator", Talking Heads.

"Tokyo", Nena (German lyrics). Most of the 18 songs on *"Definitive Collection"* could be mentioned here.

Films

There are so many movies that bring information about expanding your life. Some are just giving little hints, seeds for your further growth. As you can see, even 'old' movies having those messages.

"The Connected Universe", 2016, director: Malcolm Carter, www.theconnecteduniversefilm.com.

"Celestine Prophecy" 2007.

"What the bleep? Down the rabbit hole" (5 set DVD) 2006. (The theatrical version is limited)

"The Lord of the Rings", series.

"Battlestar Galactica", series.

"Jerry Maguire", 1996.

"Jonathan Livingston Seagull", 1973, based on a novel.

Sources

Book: N. B. Denny, *The Folklore of China and Its Affinities with that of the Aryan and Semitic Races*, London/Hongkong 1876, www.archive.org/details/cu31924023266293

Book: Li Leyi, *Tracing the roots of Chinese characters: 500 cases*, Beijing Language and Culture University Press 1994, second edition, ISBN 7-5619-0204-2

Book: Masaru Emoto, *The Hidden Messages in Water*, original in Japanese 2001.

Internet link: (Online Bible study suite): biblehub.com/

Internet link about water levels (NASA): www.giss.nasa.gov/research/briefs/gornitz_09/

Internet link about genomics (US National Library of Medicine) The Origin of Amerindians and the Peopling of the Americas According to HLA Genes: Admixture with Asian and Pacific People: www.ncbi.nlm.nih.gov/pmc/articles/PMC2874220/

www.ingramcontent.com/pod-product-compliance
Lightning Source LLC
Chambersburg PA
CBHW020104310726
48970CB00002B/478